GOD'S GREEN LINIMENT

by Lois Johnson Rew

drawings by Avis Johnson Thomas

design by Anita R. Heihn

Green Leaf Press

P.O. Box 5, Campbell, California 95009

ISBN 0-938462-02-4

Library of Congress Catalog Card Number 81-84183

Green Leaf Press, P.O. Box 5, Campbell, CA 95009

PRINTED IN THE UNITED STATES OF AMERICA

GOD'S GREEN LINIMENT

This book is for my mother,
who told me the stories

Alice Lundquist Johnson

One

"Ka-thunk." The ground rumbled and shook. "Ka-thunk, ka-thunk." A giant black machine turned from Sandy Hollow Road into the driveway of the farm. "Ka-thunk, ka-thunk, ka-thunk." Alice took one look and ran to the safety of the house. She stopped on the steps of the side porch and looked again.

"Vi, what is it?" she asked, and her voice trembled.

Eleven-year-old Viola stood up on the seat of the maple tree swing, so she could see all the way down the driveway.

"Oh, I know. It's the steam engine. Remember, Pa said the threshers would be at our house

1

tomorrow." She squinted in the glare of the hot Illinois sun. "They must be all done working at Henry Peterson's so they brought the machines down here."

Louder now, the bumpy iron wheels thumped and throbbed on the hard-packed gravel of the driveway, and the engine chugged as though it pulled a train. Suddenly a big cloud of black smoke poofed out of the funnel smokestack, and an even bigger machine came clanking around the corner behind the steam engine.

"Look." Viola let go the prickly swing rope with one hand and pointed. "Here comes the thresher. It's like a great big iron beetle. See, it's got a giant feeler that's waving at us." Alice shivered and scrunched herself on the steps to make herself smaller.

"I don't want that big beetle to wave at me," she said. "He looks like he wants to eat me."

"Don't be a baby. You can't be afraid of a machine." Vi shouted to make herself heard over the clatter and bang as the engine went by.

"I'm not a baby. I'm big enough to go to school this year!" Alice stood up and stuck out her chin. "Besides, I'm not scared. It's just the noise I don't like."

The steam engine and thresher had clanked past now, heading across the wagon yard toward the stubble field behind the big barn. The black smoke hung in the hot still air, but the noise softened as the machines moved away. Viola lowered herself to the seat again and pushed off with her feet, sending the swing high in the air and making the maple branches quiver.

"Scaredy-cat, scaredy-cat!" she taunted in her big-sister way. Alice couldn't stand it any longer. She jumped off the side porch step and ran to the back of the house and across the wagon yard to the milkhouse. She stopped at the pump and pulled down hard on the long handle with both hands—just enough to start a small stream of water which she drank out of cupped hands.

"I'll show her," she said to herself. "I'll show her I'm not a scaredy-cat. I'm gonna ask Pa if I can help with threshing tomorrow. Anyhow, I'm Pa's best helper in the barn. Better'n Vi. Everybody knows that."

The next morning both giant machines were quiet. The steam engine crouched sleepily in the center of the field behind the barn, and the iron beetle rested next to it, waiting for its first meal of golden grain. In the house Pa hurried to swallow the last bite of his breakfast. Grandpa sat at the table too. He had driven out from town early that morning to help with the threshing. Now he set his coffee cup down on the saucer and pushed back his chair. Alice's words tumbled out in a rush.

"Pa, can I help today? Can I help tramp down the strawstack? Please?" Her father was half out of his chair, but he sat back down, shaking his head.

"No, you can't be on the strawstack," he said. "You're too little. You girls stay out of the field, both of you." He looked at Ma, and she nodded her agreement.

"You can go to the fence, but no closer. It'll be noisy and dirty, and the men will be busy. They won't have time to look out for nosy little girls."

"Besides," Pa added a warning, "that long belt between the engine and the thresher is dangerous. Why, if it breaks, it could kill you!" Tears began to well up in Alice's eyes, and Grandpa turned to Pa.

"Must be somethin' the child can do. I'll be tendin' the fire, and it shoots out a lot of sparks. How about if she sits by the fence to watch for

4

sparks?"

Pa smiled. "That's a good idea. That can be your job, Alice. If you see any little fires starting, you yell like everythin'. That'll be a big help."

At these words Alice cheered up. Even if she couldn't be on the strawstack, she had a job. It wouldn't be so scary near the fence, and still she could prove to her sister that she wasn't afraid of the giant beetle, and that she truly was Pa's best helper.

"C'mon, Vi," she said, "let's go outside and watch."

Viola sniffed. "Can't. I got to stay in the house and help Ma with dinner." Her voice became a whine. "Ma, doesn't Alice have to stay in and help too? She always wants to be so big. And she's a girl. She ought to stay in the house."

Alice held her breath. Ma knew how much she liked to be Pa's helper outside, but today there was lots of kitchen work to do. Would Ma make her stay in? She sighed in relief when Ma shook her head.

"No. Pa gave her a job to do outside today, and it's an important job. Why, if that straw catches on fire, the whole farm could burn up. You go ahead, honey. After dinner you can help by clearing the table."

GOD'S GREEN LINIMENT

Without waiting any longer, Alice raced out the kitchen door. The wagon yard was already full of grown men and big boys and wagons and teams. She recognized all the neighbors from Sandy Hollow Road and some from Eleventh Street too. She saw Nels Fisk, who collected their milk everyday, and Henry Peterson, Pa's good friend. She saw the Nelsons, the Hales, Mr. Danberg, the Carlsons, the

McEvoys, and John Davidson. For a few minutes she heard a hubbub of greetings both in Swedish and English. Then, one by one, the farmers with wagons drove off to the back fields, and the other men set to work behind the barn.

Walking carefully because she was barefoot,

Alice crossed the wagon yard and went around the barn. She walked along the fence until she found a shady spot under a stump sprout. There she settled down on a mound of grass to watch. She saw Grandpa and Mr. Clemson starting a big fire in the engine firebox to make steam. Pa had told her how the thresher worked. The steam turned a big wheel on the side of the engine, and the wheel spun the big belt that Pa had said was so dangerous. The big looping belt made the thresher jaws work to separate the grain kernels from the stems.

It was still early morning, but heat waves already danced over the big machines. After a few minutes Alice looked back toward the barn and saw Viola coming.

"Thought you had to stay in the house," Alice said. "Oooh! Look at all that black smoke!" She shivered a tiny bit as Viola sat down next to her.

"Ma said I could come out to watch for a little after I dried the breakfast dishes. She's got Mrs. Hale and Mrs. Peterson to help her cook dinner." As the noise got louder, she turned to Alice. "You might as well come back to the house with me. You don't have a real job anyhow. Even if you did see a fire, who could hear you over all that noise?"

For now the steam was up. Black smoke belched out of the engine smokestack, the wheel turned, and the belt began to spin. The threshing machine started to clatter and bang and whoosh. Mr. Hale drove up next to the thresher, his hay wagon loaded high with bundles of oats. Two men leaped to the wagon with wicked-looking pitchforks and tossed the bundles into the open mouth of the thresher. ROAR-R-R. The mouth gobbled them up.

Sticky, prickly chaff and straw blew in a blizzard out of the long metal feeler and began to pile up on the ground, beginning a new strawstack. The tiny pieces of chaff hung suspended in the air in a thick green and gold cloud. Black smoke from the coal fire funneled up into the hot still air, and the whole field began to smell of heat and straw and chaff and smoke and sweat. In her little patch of shade at the fence row, Alice began to feel dizzy. Lifting her stubby braids away from her hot neck, she turned to Vi.

"How do you s'pose they know what to do?" she asked. "They don't even talk to each other." Vi smiled in her know-it-all way.

"They're grown-ups," she answered. "Nobody has to tell them what to do. Besides, they've been

9

working together all week.''

It was true that the men worked together as a smooth team, always having a wagon ready with long stalks of grain to feed into the hungry giant beetle's mouth. Two wagons with teams of horses made the trips back and forth, back and forth from the fields. When Mr. Hale's wagon was empty, he chirruped to his horses and pulled away, leaving space for Nels Fisk to pull in with Pa's loaded wagon.

Meanwhile Grandpa and Roy Clemson fed the fire that made the water boil for steam, and the oldest McEvoy boy spread the golden straw evenly with his long-tined fork and stamped it down. Pa stood in the wagon box, shoveling and smoothing the mound of grain that poured out of the thresher.

Alice watched without talking. Then she turned to ask another question, but her sister was gone. "She must've gone back to the house," she thought. She bent her head to her shoulder to wipe the sweat off her forehead onto her dress. "Whew! It's hot. Makes me feel all dizzy. Maybe I should go back too." She stared out at the giant black beetle. "No, Pa told me to watch for sparks. I better stay here."

All around her the green-gold air shimmered and throbbed like bubbling thick soup. The giant engine

10

puffed and chugged and vomited out its sooty smoke. The long curving belt whirled in a figure eight, too fast to see, and the monster machine clanked and whooshed and belched over its meal. For a long time Alice crouched in her little patch of shade. Hypnotized by the noise and heat, her head began to throb.

Then, through it all, as though from a great distance, she heard the dinner bell. Its clear Clang! Clang! slid through the thick air like a cooling stream of water. She leaped to her feet to run to the house but all at once, without warning, everything went black and her head spun dizzily. She grabbed for the fence to keep from falling. What was the matter with her head?

She hung on to the fencepost until at last the blackness cleared away, and she could see again. Then she shook her head like a dog coming out of water and tottered down the fence row toward the barn, touching each fencepost as she went. Finally her head stopped going in circles, and she climbed over the fence and trudged toward the house. The threshers had heard the dinner bell too. Alice sighed with relief. The roar of the giant machine was dying down.

Two

The deep shade under the maples felt cool after the shimmer and glare in the field, and she plopped down gratefully on the grass near the side porch. As the men straggled in from the back field, they stopped at the pump by the windmill to wash up. Ma had placed enamel washbasins, chunks of yellow soap, and old towels on a bench near the pump. Nels Fisk pulled off his straw hat and fanned himself as he waited his turn to wash.

"Whew! Must be the hottest day of the summer!" He poked Pa with his elbow. "How come it gets so hot on your farm, Fred?"

"Think it's any cooler down the road at your place, Fisk?" Pa grinned and smoothed the ends of his long curving moustache. "Here now, you hot-head, go cool off. I'll pump for you."

Mr. Fisk filled his washbasin with water and soaped his face and his neck. Then he lathered his hairy arms all the way to his elbows. He bent his head under the spigot. Pa pumped furiously, and the water gushed out, soaking Mr. Fisk's shirt halfway to his waist. He came up laughing and sputtering.

"Tryin' to drown me, hey?" He shook his head, and the flying drops sparkled. "Yah, but it feels good. Now I'll pump for you. Do you dare?" Pa laughed and ducked his head under the pump.

Each man washed up at the pump and slicked down his wet hair, squinting to see in the little mirror that dangled from a nail in the maple. Too shy to join the men, Alice sat in the cool shade and waited her turn.

Grandpa was the last one in from the field, and he walked across the wagon yard stiff-legged. His eyes squinted almost shut to keep out the bright light, and his gray-brown beard curled and crinkled, swooping right around his chin from one ear to the other. Under his nose a thick gray-brown moustache spread out to almost cover his mouth. He pulled the bandanna from around his neck.

13

"Alice," he called. "Can you come pump for me?"

"Sure I can," she answered. She ran to the pump and pulled down on the handle with both hands while he sloshed water over his face and neck. He sighed as he rubbed himself dry.

"I'm gettin' too old to work in the hot sun—even though it's easier than it used to be."

"How do you mean easier, Grandpa?"

"Why, back when I was workin' this farm, we didn't have any newfangled threshin' machines. They wasn't even invented yet. We flailed by hand. That was some job." He sighed again. "Still, it's just as well I quit farmin' and moved to Rockford. Farmin' is hard work." He tucked his bandanna in his pocket and turned to Alice. "I see you was watchin' for sparks out there. That's good. But it's hot out there, ain't it? You're all red in the face. Bend down here, and I'll pump for you."

Clean and cooled off from the water, Alice climbed the back porch steps to the hot kitchen while Grandpa joined the other men by the side porch. The kitchen had never been so busy. With a whoosh, Mrs. Hale swept past carrying an enormous platter of stewed chicken and dumplings to the

14

dining room. Alice felt like she was in the way, so she ducked into a corner, looking to see what else Ma had fixed.

The kitchen table was covered with platters and bowls waiting to be passed. Alice's mouth watered at the sight of a huge beef roast with its matching bowl of thick, rich gravy. She watched Viola stick a fork on the platter of sliced tomatoes and serving spoons in bowls of mashed potatoes and green beans. Ma stood at the cookstove fishing yellow ears of sweet corn from boiling water, and Mrs. Peterson pulled a pan of hot biscuits from the oven. Alice dodged around Viola and peeked into the dining room.

Ma's best snowy-white linen tablecloth covered the long table. Early that morning, when Ma had brought out the cloth, Alice had heard Viola say, "Ma, do you have to use the good tablecloth for threshers?"

Ma's answer had been sharp. "Our best table-cloth is none too good for men who work so hard to help us! See that you set the table as careful as if it was the preacher who was coming to dinner!"

Now the men stomped through the side door and streamed into the dining room, laughing and

15

talking. Pa took his place at the head of the long table, and all sixteen heads bowed together as Pa asked the blessing. Ma set the last big bowl on the table with a thump.

"There," she smiled, "that's all you get."

"Then we better dig in!" Pa laughed. He picked up the platter nearest him and passed it to Harry Hale.

The men piled their plates high and ate quickly, stopping their chewing only long enough to make a teasing comment or remark about the heat, the horses, or the threshing machine. When they finished, they pushed their chairs back slightly, and Ma brought the pies—apple, peach, and cherry. Each man ate two enormous pieces of pie, and then finished off his meal with a steaming cup of coffee and a toothpick for chewing.

Ma poured the coffee all around and hurried back to the kitchen where Alice and the rest of the women were eating. "You'd think it was too hot to drink coffee," she said, "but I'm sure they'll all drink more than one cup. I'm glad I borrowed your coffee pot, Grace!" She lifted the lid of the big enameled pot. "Oh, my goodness, the water's boiling already." She poured coffee beans quickly into the top of the

16

grinder and spun the handle round and round. Then she pulled open the little drawer at the bottom and measured ground coffee into a small bowl.

Mrs. Peterson looked up from her plate. "Need some help, Julia?" she asked, breaking a biscuit in two.

"No, *tack*," Ma said thanks in Swedish. "Many times as I've made Swedish egg coffee, I think I could do it in my sleep."

"What other kind of coffee is there, Ma?" Alice asked.

Ma cracked a whole egg into the bowl and stirred the sticky mixture together. Then she spooned the egg-coffee grounds into the bubbling water.

"Plain coffee, I guess you'd call it, honey. Whoops!" She quickly stirred the foaming coffee with her spoon and pushed the pot to a cooler spot on the cookstove. "It tried to climb right out of the pot that time! People who don't make egg coffee just dump the coffee grounds and water together and boil them. But it's not as good that way. It gets muddy and dark brown."

"You make the best coffee on Sandy Hollow Road, Julia," Mrs. Hale said, and Ma's face turned

17

pink with pleasure.

"I think the secret of good coffee is to add an egg." She turned to Alice. "The egg acts like a glue. It keeps the muddy bits of grounds in one big lump that stays in the pot. And besides," Ma laughed, "with egg coffee I can add water and reheat all day. Even if the pot is almost empty, the 'sump' can be thinned enough to make another cup." She looked into the dining room, calling, "Ready for more coffee, men?" Then she lifted the heavy pot in her hand and left the room.

Soon the big dinner was over, and the men stood up to go back to the field. Henry Peterson stuck his head in the kitchen door as he was leaving.

"*Tack sa mycket*, Julia," he called out, saying thank you. "Best dinner I've had in a long time!" He looked at his wife sitting at the kitchen table. "Oh, hello, Mother—didn't see you sitting there!" He laughed out loud as he slammed the door behind him.

The women sat back to relax before tackling the high stacks of sticky dishes. Ma looked at Alice and frowned.

"Goodness, honey, your face is as red as a cherry. Are you so hot as that?" She reached out her

18

hand. "Let's see if you have a fever. Mmmm. A little. It must be too hot out in the field for you. Why don't you stay in the yard this afternoon where it's shady?"

Alice gulped. "But Pa told me to watch for sparks, and . . . and Grandpa said I was doing a good job."

"I don't care what they said. There's plenty of men out there can watch for sparks. I don't want you getting heat stroke, so you stay out of the sun this afternoon." She stood up and wiped her hands on her apron, so she didn't see Viola's smirk. But Alice did.

"You girls start clearing the table," Ma said. "This kitchen is a mess!"

When Alice went back outside, the air was hotter than ever and had a clinging, heavy feeling. All the threshers had gone back to work behind the barn, and the whoosh-clatter-bang-snort of the threshing machine filled the air.

She lingered on the porch steps, breathing the prickly chaff-laden air with shallow breaths. "How different it smells when Pa is haying," she thought. "Then the air smells cool and crisp and green." Later, as the windrows of hay dried golden brown

19

under the sun, the scent became sweeter—honey sweet almost. And finally, when Pa pitched the forkfuls of hay onto the hay wagon, and Alice and Viola helped by trampling it down, the smell was dusty and dry—still sweet, but now with a grainy sweetness, like coarse brown sugar.

Threshing smelled different. For one thing, the black iron beetle-machine gave off its own smells of oil and hot metal, steam and black smoke. But oat straw and wheat straw smelled different from hay, too. The smell was thicker and not sweet. It wasn't quite gummy, but it was a sticky smell with a raspy feeling, like cockleburs.

"I like the smell of fall better," Alice thought. "The oats and wheat piled in the corn crib give off a dry and slidy smell. Straw smells good then too— clean and dry and crackly when Pa pitches it into the stalls for bedding down the horses."

But now the summer air was hot and still, and the prickly smell of threshing was more than Alice could bear. Her head felt light enough to float away, and her braids stuck to her neck like heavy ropes. Since Ma had forbidden her to go to the back field, she walked slowly across the driveway and into the spotted shade of the orchard. Here the beetle-monster's noise was softened by distance. In the middle of the orchard one branch of an apple tree crooked out sideways about ten feet from the ground. On this branch Pa had tied the ends of a stout hemp rope, first looping the rope through a hole at each end of a smooth board. The swing in the maple tree by the side porch went higher, but this apple tree swing made a good place to be alone.

Alice settled her bottom firmly on the weathered gray seat. She pushed back with her feet until she stood on tiptoe at the far edge of the worn patch of ground. Then, with a bounce of her knees and a tuck of her body, she launched the swing. It swung free over the worn patch and high up to the other side. There, heart-shaped apple leaves, greenness and coolness surrounded her. The swing paused only a little at the top of the arc and made another rush— backwards this time—to the other side. Now she looked down from a perch in the air.

Swinging was freedom. The rush of air, the choice to pump or not to pump, the swift changes between looking up into the green or down onto the brown—all these had an almost dreamy effect. Soon her thoughts traveled far away. She dreamed she was a ship (the one that had brought Pa from Sweden to

America), and she leaped from wave to wave in a dash across the sea.

"Ahoy," said Captain Alice as she swooped up into the green, "I see land far away!"

Then in her thoughts she spread strong wings and became a bird—not a clumsy black crow, but a golden hawk that balanced on the hot air currents. Catching the wind, she circled higher and higher . . . up . . . up . . . up . . .

SHR . . . I . . . EEE . . . K! BOOM! At the top of the swing's arc the sound hit her like a giant fist in the back. Letting go the prickly ropes with both hands, Alice screamed and felt herself tumbling through the air. She hit the ground crouched over, and her ankle twisted under her weight. Even as the pain stabbed, she straightened up and ran—terrified of the noise, dizzy from the swing. Limping, she ran to the very end of the orchard, to the barbed wire fence. There she threw herself face down on the long mounded grass, crying in big shuddering gasps. Her tears came hotly, and her heart pounded in her ears.

Three

Sometime later Ma's cool voice trickled into the red waves of terror. She heard her call, "Alice? Come to the house. Come here!"

When Ma called like that, Alice knew she should obey, but still she didn't budge. Here in the orchard she could feel the coarse grass and the bumpy dirt. Here she was safe. Out there somewhere a shrieking monster waited. She shivered all over, remembering the terrible noise.

At last between her sobs Alice heard firm footsteps and a swoosh of skirts. "Silly goose!" her mother scolded. "Making me walk all the way out here to get you because of a little noise. What's the matter with you, anyway?" She touched Alice on the shoulder and pulled her to her feet. "Stop your crying now, and come say good-by to Grandpa."

"Ma," Alice quavered, "what happened?"

"It was just the steam engine," Ma said. "The men are finished out in back, and they're taking the machinery to the next farm." She lifted the corner of her apron and wiped the streaky tears from Alice's face. "They all stopped at the house for some lemonade and cake, and they parked the engine and thresher in the wagon yard."

"But what was that scary noise?" Alice asked.

"The engine built up a head of steam," Ma said, "and the steam blew off all at once. That's all it was —just a big noise. Now hurry. Grandpa's hitched up and ready to go to town, and you're being silly."

At the supper table that night Alice picked at her food. She cut her meat into tiny pieces and pushed them around her plate. She drank a glass of milk because it was cool going down her aching throat, but she shook her head when Ma offered a piece of applesauce cake.

"I don't know what's gotten into that child," Ma said. "First she runs to the end of the orchard crying and won't come back. Now she won't eat

25

any supper."

Pa sat with his legs stretched out in front of him. His arm muscles twitched with weariness, and even his moustache drooped.

"Probably too much excitement in one day. I know I'm plenty tired myself. And I still got to rub down Blackie's legs with some o' that green liniment."

"Oh, Fred, do you have to do it tonight?" Ma asked. "You need to rest."

"Yah, I got to all right. He was limpin' by the time we quit workin' today, and he'll be too stiff to work tomorrow unless he's tended to. The horses are more important than me when we're workin' 'em as hard as we did today." He put his big hands on the table and slowly pushed himself to his feet.

"I'm goin' out to the barn. You better go to bed, Alice, soon's you help clear the table."

For once, Alice was glad to be sent to bed. Her face felt hot, and behind the bones around her eyes, she felt pounding. It went "clank-whoosh, clank-whoosh, clank-whoosh" like the threshing machine. She gathered up the forks and knives and brought them to the sink. Vi stacked the plates and cleared away the milk glasses.

"Were you just scared of that big noise this

afternoon, or are you sick?'' she asked.

"I wasn't scared," Alice answered, though she knew she was fibbing. "But I feel funny, and my leg hurts."

"You're all red again," Vi said. "Listen, I'll finish up tonight. I don't mind doing it by myself."

Gratefully, Alice dried her hands and slipped into the small bedroom she shared with her sister. She was too tired to wash up again, so she simply pulled off her old dress and tugged her nightgown over her head. The fiery sun was down, but the air still steamed, so she lay down on top of the quilt. Soon the clattering dishes and murmuring voices from the kitchen began to fade away. Like a prickly sweater, the hot night wrapped itself around her body, and she began to dream.

In the dream she found herself sitting on the fence at the edge of the field, watching the threshers. No blue sky arched over the farm—no puffy clouds drifted in the blue. The green and gold air thickened like scummy pond water, and little pieces of chaff floated in the thickness. She sucked in great deep breaths, but the scummy air moved toward her and pressed against her chest. Raspy pieces of chaff caught in her throat and burned.

27

GOD'S GREEN LINIMENT

Out in the green-gold world she saw her father, and she forced a cry into the thick air. "Pa! Pa! I can't breathe!" Then she stared unbelieving . . . he didn't even turn his head.

Louder than the beating of her own heart she heard the giant black beetle in the center of the field. Clank-whoosh . . . clank-whoosh . . . clank-whoosh. It opened its toothy jaws and swallowed a bundle of grain. Clank! The jaws snapped shut, tearing and chomping at the stalks. Whoosh! The beetle spat the kernels into the wagon. The engine belched out a sooty black cloud . . . clank-whoosh!

Suddenly the beetle drew itself up on its legs and began clanking its way toward Alice . . . opening its jaws and swallowing as it came. She tried to run . . . she couldn't move. Straining to see through the murky air, she called again, "Pa, Pa!" . . . but he was only a shape in the green-gold cloud. The black beetle clanked toward her . . . snapping open its enormous jaws . . . trailing its sooty cloud. A team of horses in its path reared and bolted. The wagon overturned. A man scrambled to his feet to run, but the beetle flung out a long metal arm . . . clank! . . . and the man disappeared into the mouth . . . whoosh!

Again Alice cried, "Pa! Help me!" But the

28

clanking grew so loud, she knew he couldn't hear.

In her dream the beetle was halfway across the field now, its black head nodding and grimacing as it came . . . CLANK—WHOOSH! Desperately Alice tried to lift her legs . . . to jump . . . to run. She couldn't move! She felt the creature's hot oily breath in her face, and she closed her eyes and threw up her hands to cover her ears. Even so, she heard the CLANK as the jaws opened.

Sh . . ri . . . eek BOOM! The beetle's teeth clamped down on her right leg, and the creature screamed with joy. Alice screamed too, feeling herself pulled by the leg into the cruel opening.

Then all was blackness and silence. There was nothing. For a long time there was nothing.

At last in the blackness, a new dream began, and Alice felt herself moving. She thought she must be on the swing in the orchard, swinging back and forth in short arcs over the bare oval of ground. The thick air steamed and pushed against her chest. Her throat felt tight and dry.

"Ma!" she cried. "I'm so thirsty!"

Then the blackness grayed a little, and Alice felt Ma's cool hand on her burning forehead, and some words faded in the distance . . . "Oh, Lord, please don't let her suffer so . . .''

Another hand smoothed back her sticky hair, and someone held a glass of water to her cracked lips. The water cooled the inside of her mouth, but it was hard to swallow. She stirred restlessly, and she heard someone sobbing. Then Ma's cool hand brushed her forehead once again, and the far away voices murmured.

Again Alice dreamed she sat on the rope swing in the orchard. Pushing off with her toes, she pumped hard to get up into the leafy branches. The arc of the swing was long and slow . . . no air rushed past her hot face to dry the sweat. She pumped again to make the swing go faster . . . instead, it seemed to drag. She bent over double, pulled back hard on the prickly ropes, and forced her bottom and legs straight out into the hardest pump yet . . . . Still the swing moved slowly through the air as though it moved in a pool of honey.

Push—swing—pump—swing. Straining at the ropes and pumping with all her might, Alice swung up among the cool green apple leaves. At last! She opened her lips to suck in the cooler air . . . Shr . . . i . . . eek BOOM! A mighty fist beat her on the back, pushing her off the wooden seat and into the air.

Screaming, she fell down and down, her arms and legs tumbling wildly. Thump! She hit the ground with her right leg doubled under her. Pain raced up the leg like a jagged bolt of lightning. She tried to get up and run . . . as she had run from the sound before . . . but her leg was on fire . . . she couldn't move! Off in the distance she heard someone scream.

Then, once again, the dream ended.

"Pa . . ral . . y . . sis." The word dropped syllable by syllable into the silence like water dripping slowly into a pail. "I'm afraid it's infantile paralysis. It attacks the muscles, and there's nothing I can do. Even if she survives the fever, she'll be a cripple. The muscles in this leg will be ruined."

The words meant nothing, but they sounded cold and empty and final. Alice opened her eyes to see Ma and Pa and Dr. Banks standing around her bed and staring solemnly down at her. Pa's face looked bleak and hopeless. Ma's eyes were smudged with big blue-gray circles, but she smiled as she took Alice's hot hand in her own cool one.

Then Alice drifted away. By some dream magic she changed into a leaf, spinning in its own orbit as it floated to the ground . . . spinning . . . slowly

31

spinning . . . pa . . ral . . y . . sis.

Now a lemon-colored winter sun shone through bare trees along the riverbank. In a new dream Alice hurried to buckle the double runner skates over her heavy boots, though her fingers were stiff and awkward from the cold. Viola already skated up the icy river, smoothly spinning round and round. With an impatient tug Alice pulled the last strap in place and leaped to her feet, running on the smooth ice . . . running to catch her spinning sister.

"Wait for me!" she called. "I'm coming."

She felt her skate catch on a stick frozen in the ice just as she began to fall, and she flailed her arms wildly to catch her balance. But she fell . . . the ice sagging and cracking under her. She knew the river current would pull her under the ice, so she thrashed about to stay float. But her legs slipped under the ice and into the freezing water. Strangely, only one leg seemed to be in the water . . . but even that made her so cold that she shook, her teeth banging against each other.

"Ma, I'm freezing," she cried. And that dream ended too.

The pain came and went, came and went in

flashes, as though a door from a brightly lit room opened and shut. Then the pain was always there, but the door opened and the light seemed to stay.

"I must be in Blackie's stall with Pa," Alice thought. "I can smell that green horse liniment. Poor Blackie—he's hurt his leg again."

She crinkled her nose against the stinging smell and opened her eyes. She *was* with Pa but in her bedroom, not in the horse stall. He was bending over her, and he didn't notice that her eyes were open. He poured a pool of green liniment in one hand. Then he cradled her right leg in his other big calloused hand, and slowly, gently, up and down, he began to rub her aching leg. As he rubbed, his lips moved in prayer. "Lord I'm dependin' on you . . . this child needs your help . . . stop the awful pain . . . and, Lord, end the fever . . . ." Up and down he rubbed, while the green liniment smell grew stronger. Up and down . . . "Please, God" . . . up and down.

Alice closed her eyes and slept, pushing away the pain.

Four

A big hand on her forehead and the rumble of a deep voice woke Alice from her long sleep. Stirring restlessly, she opened her eyes. Dr. Banks sat by her bed.

"That's quite a nap you had, young lady," he said, his brown eyes studying her carefully. "Two days and two nights is a long time to sleep. But you're much better today, and your fever is down." He turned to Ma. "Let's see if our patient is hungry."

"Look!" Ma smiled uncertainly and held out a saucer in her hand. "Dr. Banks brought you an ice cream cone. Isn't that a treat?"

She pulled up a chair and sat next to Alice, spooning the ice cream from the saucer and feeding

34

her as though she were a baby. The cracker cone tipped to one side of the mushy mound like a long pointed hat. The caramel ice cream had partly melted, and it dripped off the spoon, but the creamy sweetness slid easily down Alice's throat.

"Brought that ice cream all the way from the drugstore on Seventh Street, so it's a little soft," Dr. Banks chuckled and folded his arms across his chest. "Almost dropped it when I made the turn onto Sandy Hollow Road, what with trying to manage the horse and all. But I juggled a little and made it all right. Does it taste good?"

Alice looked at the doctor gratefully. "Thank you," she murmured between spoonfuls.

"I believe she's hungry," Ma said, "and it's no wonder. Sick as she's been, she hasn't eaten for half a week."

Half a week? Where had she been all that time? The last thing Alice remembered was climbing up on the bed on threshing day—her head throbbing. And then the dreams came. She shuddered at the thought of the dreams, and the mattress under her swayed and creaked. She looked down, surprised. She was in her bedroom all right, but she was not in bed. Instead, she was lying in the old high-wheeled wicker baby buggy. She had been too big for it for years, and it had been put away in the upstairs storeroom. Anxiously she looked at her mother's face.

"Ma, am I dreaming?" she asked.

"No, honey, this time you're not dreaming. I think you had some bad dreams while you were sick, but this is real." Ma's hand shook a little, and the spoon rattled against the saucer.

"But why am I in the baby buggy?" Alice looked around again and saw that the wicker end of the buggy had been broken out, and her legs stuck through the broken place. Over at the window, the doctor cleared his throat.

"You've been a very sick little girl, and the heavy blankets hurt your legs," he said. "Your pa put you in there so he could prop up the blankets and still keep you warm."

Ma scraped the last bit of ice cream from the saucer, and Alice let her heavy head fall back on the pillow. Her right leg ached with a steady, throbbing pain, and her arms and chest felt weighted down. She watched through half-closed eyes as her mother pushed the chair back and turned to face the doctor.

"What do you think?" Ma asked in a shaky kind of voice.

"I think the crisis is over. Her fever's down, and obviously she's no longer delirious."

A look of joy passed like a sunbeam over Ma's tired-looking face. "It's the answer to prayer," she said.

"I don't know what you and Fred did for her, Julia," the doctor went on, "but it must have been the right thing." Ma stood up and went to the window.

"I'm not sure how to tell you," she began in a low voice, "because I don't suppose you're going to like it. We've—we've been rubbing her leg with horse liniment!"

"Horse liniment?" The doctor's eyebrows rose with the question.

"Yes, horse liniment." Ma stopped a minute and then continued. "We rubbed her with alcohol like you said, until the alcohol was gone. Then Fred drove into town to buy some more."

"And—?" The doctor's voice was very deep.

"And we'd forgotten it was Sunday. There wasn't any place at all that would sell Fred alcohol on a Sunday."

"Ah, I hadn't thought of that," the doctor said.

"Fred rang me on the telephone. We were frantic

37

to do something—anything—because Alice was screaming so. I told him to buy some kind of liniment that had a lot of alcohol in it. Fred thought right away of the green liniment he uses for his horses when they're lame. When he came home, he'd bought a big bottle."

Alice was getting sleepy now, but she desperately wanted to hear what Ma and the doctor were saying. She closed her eyes to a tiny slit, but concentrated all her energy on staying awake to listen. Ma went on.

"I didn't much like the idea of using horse liniment, but the label on the bottle said it could be used for humans. And we had to do something—you know how red and feverish Alice was when you were here, and how she screamed. Even the alcohol rubs hadn't helped."

Ma paused and then went on in a rush. "The directions read: 'First rub the affected part with liniment. Then sprinkle cotton batting with water and liniment and wrap affected part well.'"

"And that's what you did?" the doctor asked.

"That's right. We rubbed the liniment on, and then we wrapped her leg in a piece of an old quilt with liniment and water on it. A few minutes later Alice complained she was freezing. Her teeth chattered and she shook so hard she even moved the buggy. But in a little while—thank God—she fell asleep, and she's been sleeping ever since. Look—she's asleep again now."

But Alice wasn't asleep, though her eyelids drooped with weariness. She heard the doctor's deep voice again.

"Good. I'm glad she's sleeping. I want to examine her leg, and I don't want to frighten her. I don't think you hurt her any by using that green horse liniment. It may even have helped to bring down the fever. But now that the fever has broken, I wouldn't use it any more."

As he talked, the doctor lifted the covers away from Alice's leg. "We don't know much about infantile paralysis, but our latest information is that it's best to keep the leg absolutely still. Some doctors even use splints to keep the limbs straight. It doesn't look like this leg is twisting, though, so I don't think that's necessary. But you'll have to keep her from moving around. That's the only hope for the leg to get better—to keep it quiet."

Through nearly closed eyes Alice watched the doctor's hands. He lifted her right leg up and cupped her heel in his big hand.

39

"Let's see if she has any feeling in this leg," he said.

With his other hand he scratched on his trouser leg with a long kitchen match. The match flared and then burned steadily with a bright flame. He brought

40

the flame close to the bottom of her foot and held it there a long time. What was he doing?

"Oh, stop! Stop it, please!" Ma screamed. "I smell her flesh burning!" She pulled the doctor's arm away.

Alice felt nothing—no burning, no heat—only the steady throbbing pain in her leg. But for a long time she remembered the fear in Ma's voice.

Five

After the doctor's visit, the days ran together into weeks—like raindrops on the window glass. Two whole months went by, but the separate days were blurred by tiredness and the constant pain in her leg. Only the pain seemed real.

One morning, though, Alice opened her eyes, and for the first time in many weeks she noticed the reddish glow of sunshine pouring into the room. Surprised, she raised herself on her elbows.

"What makes the sunshine that red color?" she wondered, squinting to see through the lace curtains. "Oh! The maple—it's the maple leaves turning! What fun it'll be to collect the prettiest red and gold leaves to bring to school . . . School!" All at once her stomach lurched, and her fingers clutched at the edge of the quilt.

"Vi! Vi!" she called, and at the end her words rose to a shriek. Her sister raced into the room, one arm halfway into the sleeve of a sweater.

"What's the matter?"

"Vi, it's time for school to start! Look, the maple leaves are red. I got to get up and go to school!" The words tumbled out on top of one another, and she threw back the covers and sat up. But the room spun in circles, and she swayed. Through the dizzy blackness, she felt her sister's steadying hand.

"Ma!" Vi called. "Alice needs you quick!"

In an instant Ma knelt by the bed and eased her whirling head onto the pillow. "What is it?" she asked.

"School—I got to go to school."

"Oh, honey, don't you see?" Ma said. "You're too sick to go to school." She caught her lower lip between her teeth and then continued. "I didn't want to tell you, but Viola started school a month ago."

"Did you—did you really?" As her head cleared, Alice looked up at her sister. Viola nodded solemnly.

43

"But when can I go?" Alice demanded. "Can I go next week when I'm well?"

Ma said nothing, but tears brimmed up in her eyes. Alice looked at her mother's face, and the lump of fear in her stomach grew and grew.

"You mean I *can't* go?" She choked out the words.

"It's because of your leg, Alice." Ma's answer was only a whisper. "The doctor says you have to stay quiet in bed to rest that bad leg."

At once Alice's hands went to her throbbing leg. It lay there, heavy and unmoving—aching.

"You . . . you mean, I can't get up even?" Wide-eyed, she stared at her mother's face.

Again Ma said nothing. Slowly she shook her head, and a single tear spilled over and ran down her cheek. She reached out and held Alice tight in her arms, but Viola, stifling a sob, ran from the room.

For several days after that Alice lay numbly in the little brass bed and stared at the ceiling. She heard the rattle of the stove lid, the ka-chump of the cistern pump, and Ma's brisk footsteps moving back and forth in the kitchen. But she lay as still as a corncob.

Gradually the numbness began to wear off. A

plan began to take shape in her mind. Half awake and half asleep she thought about the events of the past few weeks. She remembered how her heart had pounded in fear when the monster beetle threshing machine had turned into the driveway, and how she'd run to the side porch. She especially remembered her sister's taunts: "Scaredy-cat! Scaredy-cat!"

She had decided then that she wouldn't let herself be afraid: that she would make herself go out in the field by that monster machine. And she'd done it— in her mind she could still smell the chaff and smoke and heat and feel the sweat under her braids.

"And Pa gave me that job watching for sparks," she thought, " 'cause I wasn't a scaredy-cat. Grandpa even said I was good at it."

For as long as Alice could remember she'd wanted to be big—to be grown-up and go to school. When she was little, she'd watched Viola tromp down the road with her schoolbooks and her lunch pail, and she'd pretended that she was going along. Now she was finally old enough to have her own tin pail and her own schoolbooks, and now she was stuck in bed! She sighed and shifted restlessly on her pillow. What was it the doctor had said?

She thought back to the day the doctor had lit

45

the long kitchen match standing here by her bed, and she sorted carefully through the words that he'd said.

"Green horse liniment . . ." she remembered. "Paralysis . . . what a funny sounding word . . . keep the limbs straight . . . I'm afraid . . . keep her in bed."

Afraid! That was it. The doctor was afraid. But she wasn't afraid, and she was determined to get up so she could go to school. Carefully she lifted her head from the pillow—up, up slowly. So far so good. She wasn't even dizzy. Now she pulled her arms under her and pushed herself up on her elbows until she was half sitting up. Outside the window a robin flashed by, his wings a whirr against the bright maple leaves.

"I'll do it," she said to herself. "I'll show them I'm not a scaredy-cat. I'll get up, and I'll walk around, and then Ma will let me go to school."

After breakfast the next day Ma pushed an extra pillow behind her back.

"That'll raise you up a little higher," she said, "and it'll be easier for me to comb and braid your hair. I declare—you've got a little sparkle in your eyes this morning, honey. Are you feeling better?" Alice ran her fingers along the edge of Ma's apron.

"Oh, yes, Ma. I'm getting better. Maybe pretty soon I can get up and go to school." Ma sighed and tugged a little on Alice's stubby braid.

"Well, I'm praying that you will. But the doctor said you have to keep still, you know. Tell you what. I'll bring in my big button box, and you can play with the buttons this morning. Won't that be fun?"

Alice nodded. The button box was a wonderful treasure, and it was a special treat to be able to sort and arrange the heaps of buttons by color or size or in rows. Alice could use the buttons for all kinds of pretend games, and often on rainy or snowy days she'd begged Ma for the button box. But now her mind was on getting up—walking—going to school.

A few minutes later Ma brought in the button box and set it on the bed.

"There you are," she said smiling. "I'm going outside to the garden for a little while. It's time to start digging the carrots and putting them in sand for the winter. But you can see the garden from here, and if you need me for anything important, you can call." She stepped to the window and raised it a few inches. "We had frost last night, and there's a nip in the air, but the sun will keep your room warm."

As soon as Alice heard the entry way door slam, she pushed the button box to one side.

"I'm not afraid," she told herself. "I'm going to

47

get up and walk around." Carefully she sat up and turned back the heavy patchwork quilt. She twisted on the bed to bring her legs over the edge. The right leg—the one that ached so much—seemed heavy, as though it didn't belong to her body, but she used her hands to push it off the bed. Finally both legs dangled over the edge.

"I got to be careful," she thought. "I've been in bed a long time, and I don't want to get dizzy again." She rested for several minutes, sitting on the edge of the bed and enjoying the patterns of sunlight on the wood plank floor. Finally she pushed herself up and stood, her weight on the good leg.

"Now," she said to herself, "I'll show that doctor I'm not afraid to walk around."

Just like she always did, but more carefully because it ached, she stepped forward onto her right leg. At once a flashing pain stabbed from her toes to her hip. The leg crumbled under her like a rotten log, and she felt herself falling.

"Ma!" She screamed the word out as she pitched forward, hitting her head on the bureau. Behind her the button box fell. It burst open with a crash, and hundreds of buttons rolled and clattered around her.

Something cold and wet lay on her forehead. She felt a drop of water slide down into her ear, and she opened her eyes.

"Praise the Lord!" Ma stood by the bed, looking down at her with big round eyes. Alice was back in her bed under the quilt. Her head throbbed under the soggy towel, and her leg burned with pain.

"Ma, what happened?"

"I don't know, honey. I heard you scream—did you drop the button box and then fall out of bed?" Ma leaned forward and lifted the wet cloth, gently exploring the big bump on Alice's head.

"I—" Then Alice remembered. "I tried to walk, and my leg wouldn't work."

"Oh, Alice." Ma turned away and her shoulders shook.

"The doctor said he was afraid, but I'm not a scaredy-cat. I want to go to school. And I want to help Pa out in the barn like I used to. But how come my leg wouldn't work, Ma?" Her back still turned away, Ma took a deep breath. Then she slowly turned around.

"Alice, you say you want to be grown-up. All right, I'm going to tell you the truth, and you'll have to be grown-up enough to understand it." She walked

49

back to the bed and sat down on the edge.

"The doctor says there's something wrong with your leg—something called infantile paralysis. That's what made you so sick at threshing time, and that's why your leg hurts." She stopped for a minute and took Alice's hand in hers. "Now you have to rest the muscles in that leg so they'll get better. You can't try to get up. If you fall again and twist your leg funny, the doctor will put sticks of wood on each side of your leg to keep it stiff and straight." Ma looked out the window as the wind tossed red and gold maple leaves against the glass.

"This time it's not enough for you to be brave and want to walk. This time you've got to depend on God to make your leg well again. I don't know any other way." As Alice stared at her, she bent her head and closed her eyes. "Let's pray about it," she said.

"Dear God," she prayed, as she held Alice's hands tight in her own, "we ask for your help again. Please heal Alice's leg and help her to be well."

"And—and, please, God," Alice's lips moved soundlessly, "let me be grown-up and go to school."

Six

Threatened with having her leg tied to sticks of wood if she twisted it again, Alice gave up her plans to walk. Gloomily, day after day she lay propped up with pillows in her little bedroom off the sitting room. She watched the leaves of the maple tree let go one by one and drop to the ground, until by the end of November, the branches were bare and empty.

At Thanksgiving time Ma stuffed and roasted a fat chicken, and Grandpa drove out from Rockford in his little buggy to share in the dinner. Alice had to stay in bed. She mumbled grace before she ate, but she could think of little to be thankful for. God seemed to be very cold and far away.

51

GOD'S GREEN LINIMENT

A few days after Thanksgiving the first heavy snow covered the ground. Just before breakfast Pa stomped through the kitchen and into her room. His cheeks were red with cold, and his moustache bristled.

"Didja see all the snow that fell last night, little one?" He pulled the curtains from the window. "Look out there—the whole world is white!" Then he whirled around and tossed a ball at Alice. She reached up and caught it.

"Ooooh! Pa, it's cold. It's a snowball!" She giggled and dropped it on the quilt in surprise. Pa laughed.

"Thought we'd have our first snowball fight o' the winter. You better give it back though, or it'll melt in a puddle and then Ma'll be mad." He pushed up the bedroom window and tossed the snowball outside. Then he stood at the window for a minute, smoothing the waxy ends of his beautiful moustache. The sun reflected off the snow and gleamed on his soft brown hair.

"Ummm. Have to go to town today, snow or no snow. Might as well get out the cutter. This is no weather for a buggy or a wagon." He grinned at Alice. "And it's kinda fun in the first snow anyhow."

"Oh, Pa, I wish I could go too!" Alice cried.

52

"I love to ride in the cutter."

"I know," he answered, "but for now you got to be content to stay in bed." His eyes narrowed thoughtfully. "I got me a plan though . . . " Then his voice quickened. "I'll drive past your window so you can wave at Nellie," he said. "There's enough snow on the yard so it won't hurt any. But I got to hurry. I got secret business on Seventh Street."

Pa had been very mysterious about his secret business in Rockford, and though Alice asked Ma what the secret business was, Ma only smiled and shook her head. All day Alice listened anxiously for the bells on Nellie's harness. At last she heard the faint tinkle get louder and louder, and then—right outside the window—Pa stopped the cutter. As soon as she looked, Alice understood the secret.

"A fir tree, a fir tree," she sang. "Pa's bought a Christmas tree!"

A fir tree was a special treat because it had to be bought in town. Not a single fir tree grew on Sandy Hollow Farm, not even in the woodlot. Imagine, buying a tree! Pa lifted the fir tree out of the cutter and leaned it against the trunk of the maple. Then he waved to Alice and drove off in a shower of snow.

A few minutes later he came in after unhitching

Nellie. He carried a bulky paper-wrapped parcel,
and his overcoat pockets bulged with round and
square bumps. Alice held up her arms for a big hug,
but he stopped in the doorway.

"Hold on a minute!" he laughed. "I got too
many secrets to be hugged." He tossed the big
package on the bed and disappeared through the
doorway.

"What's in the package?" she asked when he
came back without his overcoat. Vi was home from
school, and she followed him into the room.

"Let us see, Pa," she said.

He broke the string and unwound the paper.
"It's *lutefisk*," he said. "Don't it look good? We're
goin' to have *lutefisk* for supper on Christmas Eve.
Thank the Lord we can live so well."

"Oh, good," Vi said, "I like *lutefisk*."

But Alice was disappointed. "It's all hard and
yellow," she said. "What is it, anyhow?"

"I thought you knew," Pa answered. *"Lutefisk*
is a big cod fish that lives in the cold water of the
Baltic Sea around Sweden. Swedish fishermen catch
the fish and dry it. Then they ship it to America
so all the Swedes here in the states can eat their
favorite fish at Christmas!"

"We can't eat it this way though," Viola picked up a hard chunk. "It looks like a stick of wood."

"That's why I bought it early." Pa tapped the stick of fish on the bedpost. "Ma will soak it in a crock with wood ashes and water to make lye. The lye will turn the fish pure white and spongy. Then she'll soak it in clear water until the lye is washed away. It takes almost a month to get *lutefisk* ready to eat on Christmas Eve."

That month before Christmas seemed never to end. Until December 24 Pa kept the fir tree outside the window in the cold air to keep it fresh. Finally, Christmas Eve day he anchored it in a bucket of sand and brought it in the house.

"You can string popcorn on strings for decoration," he said to Alice, "and Viola can hang 'em on the tree."

"But Pa, I can't even see the tree now that it's in the house!" Alice's words rose in a wail.

"I know, but you do your part, and I promise you'll get to see the decorated tree."

So that afternoon Alice sat in bed pushing a big needle through fluffy kernels of popcorn until she had a long white string full. Meanwhile Viola decorated the fir branches with shiny bits of paper and with tiny candle stubs, each in a metal holder that clipped on to the branch. Alice couldn't see the tree, but she could hear her sister as she worked in the combination sitting room-dining room.

"A fir tree grows just right for candles, doesn't it, Ma?" Viola said. "See, each branch finds its own place for poking out, and that way no candle flame has to burn under another branch."

"That's right," Ma spoke from the kitchen. "But it's still dangerous when the candles are lit, and there'll be no racing around to knock the tree over. We don't want a fire on Christmas!"

In her room Alice gulped. How she wished she could race around! As if in reminder, her useless leg gave an unpleasant twinge.

Christmas Eve! In spite of herself Alice was excited. Would Santa Claus find his way to Sandy Hollow Farm to fill the stockings? Would there be packages under the tree? What had made those bumps in Pa's pockets? What was Pa's plan?

Viola wandered in from the kitchen. She tossed her glossy brown braids over her shoulder, and her eyes snapped with excitement.

"The *lutefisk's* boiling in the kitchen, Al. Now

it's all white and swelled up just like Pa said it would be. It smells good. Can you smell it in here?" She leaned on the end of the bed. "Grandpa just came, and I get to set the table fancy for Christmas. Ma's even got the good white tablecloth out."

"How does the tree look?" Alice begged. "Are there any presents under it?" She twisted impatiently on the bed.

"No, no presents except the ones we got for Ma and Pa," Viola shook her head. "But the tree's beautiful. The candle holders and the shiny paper are sort of sparkly pink from the reflection of the fire. And Ma said we can light the candles after supper."

Alice clenched her teeth. Vi acted like she knew everything about Christmas. She'd decorated the tree, and Alice hadn't even seen it. What if Santa didn't come? What if there were no presents? Off here in the bedroom, she felt like she was in a box.

"Viola," Ma called, "come and stir the *gröt* before it burns."

"Mmm. *Gröt*—be right there, Ma." Viola disappeared around the corner.

"Push the pan to the back more," Alice heard Ma say to Vi. "The fire's not so hot back there. Rice and milk mixed together burn faster than anything

57

else I know of. *Tack*. Now you can finish setting the table.''

How Alice hated being stuck away in the corner! She could smell the good Christmas smells, and she could hear everybody talking, but she couldn't take part. She wished she could at least see the tree. A few minutes later Pa swooshed into the bedroom, bringing with him a crisp outdoor smell.

''Now, little one,'' he said, ''seems to me that for a special time like Christmas Eve we can get you up out o' that bed—no matter what the doctor says. Ma's got the sofa in the sitting room all fixed up for you. You can sit there and see the tree and have supper with us too. Does that sound good?''

Alice nodded, not trusting herself to speak. She could hardly wait to get out of bed. Pa bent down and gently lifted her in his arms. But in spite of his gentleness, her legs dangled down and she winced with pain as he carried her through the door. Her leg hurt so!

The dining room was aglow with warmth and good smells, and Alice caught her breath as she saw the fir tree. The double doors to the parlor were closed to keep out the cold, and the decorated tree stood in front of them, reaching nearly to the ceiling.

Her popcorn ropes hung like ribbons of snow on the branches, and the tin candle holders reflected both an orangy glow from the big lamp over the table and a flicker of pink from the flames in the stove. Pa settled Alice gently against the pillows on the sofa and pulled a shawl over her legs. She sighed with pleasure and pain.

GOD'S GREEN LINIMENT

"Well, young'un," Grandpa turned away from the shiny nickel parlor stove and rubbed his hands together, "it's good to see you out o' that bed. I never did believe in keepin' a little filly shut up in a stall all winter long. Are you ready for some o' your Ma's good *lutefisk*?"

Again Alice nodded. She bent sideways on the sofa, trying to see past the table. Were any other presents under the tree? Pa caught her looking and laughed.

"What are you lookin' for, little one? You know Christmas don't come until after supper."

Still, she could see some big packages tucked way back under the branches. What could they be?

Soon Pa, Ma, Viola, and Grandpa gathered at the holiday table. A bowl of boiled potatoes steamed next to a big bowl of flaky *lutefisk*. Bits of onion and butter floated in creamy white sauce in the gravy boat. Pa pulled his spindle-backed chair up to the table and bowed his head.

"Lord, we thank you for this food you have given us. And we thank you for our health and the strength to work. Tonight, Lord, we thank you for Jesus whose birth we celebrate . . ."

Alice squirmed under the shawl as Pa's prayer

went on and on. How could he thank God for good health when she couldn't even walk? And why didn't he hurry?

" . . . Amen." Pa opened his eyes and turned to Alice. "Is something wrong that makes you wiggle so?"

"No, Pa," Alice answered in a whisper.

"Then sick or not, you should be able to sit still when we're talking to God!" His words thundered in her ears.

Ma fixed a big plate and brought it to Alice to set on her lap. She wasn't hungry, but she knew she had to eat. What kind of presents were under the tree? She peeked at the tree again. Good as it was to be eating with the family, she longed for the meal to end.

At last Ma cleared away the plates and brought dessert—small sauce dishes of Swedish *gröt*. Usually Alice loved this cinnamon-flavored rice and milk mixture, but tonight it stuck in her throat.

"Ma, I'm full. I can't eat any," she wailed.

"Then we can't open presents." Ma's answer was firm. "And Santa can't come to fill stockings. He'll know if you don't eat your supper."

"I finished mine already," Viola smirked.

"Santa will bring my presents, won't he, Ma?"
"Yah, I guess he will. You start cleaning up the kitchen. We can open the presents under the tree if Alice finishes her supper." Ma hurried to the kitchen, leaving Alice fidgeting on the sofa.

Still half a bowl of *gröt* to eat! She sent a stricken look toward Pa. She was already in his bad graces for wriggling during the prayer. If she didn't eat, she'd really be in trouble. But as soon as Ma turned her back, Pa winked—a slow deliberate wink. Then he pushed his chair back. Reaching over to Alice's bowl, he heaped up his own spoon. Swiftly he popped the *gröt* into his mouth and swallowed. He grinned as Ma came back.

"Well, Mother, she's almost done. Seems like Christmas is just about here!"

Santa Claus came to fill the stockings late at night when everyone was asleep. But on Christmas Eve there were always a few family presents under the tree. These presents were opened before bedtime while the candles on the fir tree were lit for the first time. That's what Pa meant by "Christmas is almost here."

Now Ma scratched a long kitchen match and moved around the tree, lighting the tiny candles. Alice squinted so that each glowing flame was surrounded by a halo of golden light. She caught her breath at the beauty of it. Then Vi broke the enchantment.

"Pa, can I pass out the presents now?" she asked. Pa nodded his head.

63

"Yah, go ahead. But be careful not to knock into the tree."

"Here, Al." Viola brought a big soft package and laid it on Alice's lap. "This one has your name on it. And there's one just like it for me." She moved importantly from person to person, until each had a package of some kind. Then she reached far under the tree and pulled out two small square packages. "Oooh! These are heavy. There's one for Alice and one for me. I wonder what they can be?"

"Why don't you girls open 'em right away?" Pa suggested.

"Yah," Grandpa's rocker creaked as he shifted it closer to the little stove, "it's gettin' late, and we got to get up early for *Julotta* services at church tomorrow."

Alice shook her heavy square package, and it rattled. Viola poked hers through the paper. "It's bumpy and holey, and it has little legs. What could it be?" she wondered. They pulled the paper away at the same time.

"It's a bank!" Both girls cried out together.

"They're just like real little safes," Pa said. "Remember when I wouldn't let you hug me, Alice? I had 'em in my pocket, and I didn't want you to

64

know."

Alice looked at her bank. It was heavy cast iron with a real door on the front and a slot for coins on its burnished top. Scrolly leaves decorated the door and the top of the safe, and coppery edges highlighted the dull black color.

"See the numbers on the silver knob?" Pa asked. "Each safe has a secret combination. Afterwards I'll show you how they work."

Alice shook her bank, and it rattled again. Putting her eye to the slot at the top, she caught the wink of light on copper.

"There's pennies in it too! Oh, thank you, Pa."

Pa looked serious for a minute. "Do you know why we give presents to each other? It's because God gave a present to us on the first Christmas. That present was his own son, Jesus. That's why we can be so happy and say *God Jul* to each other."

Alice smiled. She knew Pa was saying "Merry Christmas" in Swedish.

The children surprised Ma with a new potholder knitted from scraps of heavy yarn by Vi. They had pooled their pennies, and Ma had shopped for them, so Pa and Grandpa each opened a package of red bandanna handkerchiefs.

65

"Red!" Grandpa said. "Never saw red handkerchiefs before."

"Must be to keep our noses warm on these cold winter days." Pa laughed and stroked the waxy ends of his beautiful moustache. "Now Alice you should open your other present," he said. She set her bank down and pulled the paper from the soft package on her lap. Then she sucked in a deep breath.

"It's a new Sunday School dress!" she cried. It lay in soft blue folds, light and smooth under her fingers, but with the woolly feel of a warm peach on a summer afternoon. "Oh, Ma," she said, "It's beautiful!"

Until now her best dress had been a hateful maroon thing—an outgrown dress of Viola's that itched. Every Sunday when she'd been well she'd worn that dress to Sunday School. She'd clenched her teeth everytime Ma did up the tiny buttons, but she knew it would do no good to complain. Each girl had only one good winter dress, over which she wore a big white apron in the house. But Ma must have known how Alice felt about that muddy maroon thing, because this dress was the color of the sky on an April morning—a blue clear and soft with just a hint of silver. Then, suddenly, Alice's eyes filled with tears.

"But, Ma," she cried, and her words caught in a giant sob, "if I can't go out, I can't wear my new dress to church tomorrow!" Ma reached over and patted her hand.

"That's true, honey. But you're not always going to be sick, and you did need a new dress. The maroon was getting too small for you. Even though you've been in bed, you've been growing fast. Pretty soon you won't fit into Viola's old things."

Alice sighed. What good was a new dress she couldn't wear?

Next was Vi's turn, and she too opened a soft, flat package. It was another dress, longer and bigger than Alice's, and in a rusty orange that glowed like a candle next to Vi's dark braids.

"Another new dress! I'll have to wear my best hat to take such a fancy young lady to church tomorrow," Pa chuckled. "Do you think you'll be dressed too fancy to ride in the cutter?"

"Oh, Pa, stop teasing!" Vi said, tossing her head.

But Alice's heart sank. Vi was going to church services with Pa tomorrow! She would be able to show off her new dress to her friends. It wasn't fair.

Now the candles on the fir tree were burning

67

low. "Better put 'em out before the whole tree burns," Grandpa said. Ma nodded, and she quickly stepped around the tree, pinching off the tiny flames with her fingers. The sitting room seemed to lose its happy glow.

"Time for bed, girls," Pa said. "We got to be up at four o'clock in the morning for the *Julotta* service at church." He laughed. "Christmas Day is one time even city people get up early in the morning."

"Don't forget our stockings," Viola pleaded, "for Santa when he comes tonight."

"Oh, that's right," Pa smiled. "Viola, you hang one of your stockings on the back of a kitchen chair and one for Alice. Hurry now!"

He bent over Alice and lifted her in his arms. She was tired and sad, and her leg throbbed and ached. She buried her face in Pa's collar and began to sob. She couldn't help it.

The next thing she knew, Pa set her down with a jolt on the bed. His strong hands grabbed her shoulders and shook them.

"Now listen to me, little one," he said, and his voice was rough and broken. "I won't have you feeling sorry for yourself."

"But Pa," she wailed, "I can't go to *Julotta*. I

68

can't go to school. I can't help you in the barn. I can't even walk around!"

"Yah, I know all that." A deep furrow creased his forehead. "Now you got to be more grown-up than you ever been before. You got to learn patience." He sighed and rubbed his knuckles over his eyes. "Do you know what that is?"

Numbly, Alice shook her head to say no.

Pa sat still for a moment. "Late as it is, I guess the best way to tell you is to read you a story. Here, wipe your eyes." He handed her a handkerchief and then he stood up and went into the sitting room. When he returned, the big Bible was in his hands. He sat down heavily on the bed.

"Remember about Abraham?" he asked. "God promised Abraham that he'd be the father of as many people as there are stars in the sky. But poor Abraham and Sarah his wife got older and older, and they never had even one child. Still Abraham believed that God would keep his promise, so he just kept waitin'." He turned the pages. "Finally Abraham was a hundred years old . . . "

"Older than Grandpa?"

Pa nodded. "Lots older than Grandpa, but he still was willin' to wait for God. And then one day an

69

angel came to visit Abraham, and the angel said . . . Let's see . . . ah! here it is."

> "Is anything too hard for the Lord? At the appointed time I shall return to you, in the spring, and Sarah shall have a son."

"And the story goes on in Genesis. Sure enough, when spring came, those two old folks had a baby. They named him Isaac, and he was the start of a whole nation. But it took patience—bein' willing to wait. That's what patience is. Now do you understand?"

"I think so, Pa."

"Good. There's one more thing you need, and that's faith. You got to believe that God hears us prayin', and he's goin' to do somethin' about it. You got to believe that somehow you're goin' to walk again." He pulled on the end of his moustache. "Faith is sorta like the pennies in that bank. You can't see 'em from the outside, but you know they're in there."

Alice sighed. "All right, Pa."

"And besides," he continued, "maybe Santa will bring a surprise tomorrow. One that'll help you

70

move around a little."

She looked up. "What do you mean?"

He didn't answer at all, but he leaned over and kissed her on the cheek. "*God Jul*, little one," he said.

"*God Jul*, Pa," Alice whispered.

Eight

"Good morning!" Alice heard Ma's voice off in the cold distance, and she opened her eyes. The room was dark, but she could see a glow from the sitting room lamp. Closing her eyes she burrowed deeper under the warm quilt, and then she heard Ma again.

"Viola, wake up. What a sleepyhead you are. It's four o'clock. Time to get ready for church."

Viola groaned. "It's too early to get up for church," she said, and she groaned again.

"*God Jul*," Ma said. "Did you forget today was Christmas?"

Christmas! Alice's eyes flew open. "Did Santa come, Ma? Did he?" she called. She sat up in bed and shivered as the icy air of the bedroom coiled around her.

Ma came to the bedroom doorway. "I did see some lumpy stockings on the chair in the kitchen. But you go back to sleep, Alice. Pa and Grandpa are taking Vi to *Julotta* services, so there'll be no stockings till after they get back and have breakfast."

Alice's heart sank. So long to wait! And she wouldn't have the fun of riding to town in the cold crisp blackness of Christmas morning.

She remembered the early morning ride last Christmas. Pa had bundled her next to Viola in the back seat of the bobsled, and he'd tucked a warm brick in the straw at their feet. Then he'd pulled a big scratchy blanket up around them until only their noses peeked out. With all that, it was still cold! But the stars had shone, and the harness bells had jingled merrily. It had been glorious fun to be out so early in the morning.

Now she shivered again and pulled the quilt around her shoulders. "I wish I could go," she said. "It's not fair!"

Ma frowned a little and turned away. "Here, Viola, I got your clothes all ready. Run behind the sitting room stove where it's warm and get dressed.

Pa's harnessing up, so you have no time to waste."

In the cold dark of her little bedroom Alice pouted and began to feel the tears coming. Then she remembered the story about Abraham. What was it Pa had said?—Patience, learning to wait. She sighed and burrowed into the pillow. Just then she heard a curious bumping and thumping sound coming from the kitchen, and she heard Grandpa's voice.

"Wait a minute, Fred. I'll have to move the table out o' the way. There—that'll do it."

Silence again. She strained to hear, but the murmuring voices were too soft. What were they doing? She heard Pa laugh softly.

". . . big secret," he said.

Then suddenly footsteps came through the sitting room. Pa's overcoated figure filled the doorway, almost shutting out the light from the big lamp over the table.

"*God Jul*, little *Svenska flicka*," he said, calling her a Swedish girl. "Grandpa says to say goodbye. You get a little nap, and when Vi and I come back, we'll have a surprise." Alice held out her arms.

"You mean our stockings?" she asked. Pa laughed, bending down with a kiss. His moustache ends tickled her ear.

74

Then he was gone, but her tears were gone too. The words sang in her mind. Surprise, surprise, surprise. What was the surprise? She'd never be able to sleep until they got back.

But she did sleep. Before she knew it, she heard the entryway door slam.

"Ooooh, Ma!" Viola nearly shouted the words. "I'm so cold I think I'm an icicle. I got to get behind the stove where it's warm." Again Alice sat up in bed, pushing the useless leg over with her left foot. She heard Ma's quick footsteps.

"You made it back sooner than I expected. I still got to make the pancake batter. Here, hang your muffler in front of the oven so it can dry. It's all icy from your breath."

"Vi," Alice called, for she could wait no longer, "what's the surprise? Come tell me!" Viola came into the little bedroom. Her cheeks were shiny red from the cold. She ran to the bed.

"Can't tell. Here, feel how cold my fingers are?" She touched Alice on the cheek.

"Go away. You're colder than a snowball. What's the surprise? Please tell me!"

"Oh, I know, but you don't!" Viola laughed wickedly and spun away from the bed and out the

75

door.

"You're mean!" Alice shouted. Then she heard the entry door slam again.

"Where's the little girl who wants a surprise?" Pa was in from the barn with Nellie unhitched and stabled. He peered into the bedroom, and his blue eyes sparkled. "Is this the little girl I'm lookin' for?"

Alice forgot herself and gave a little bounce on the bed. A sharp pain traveled from her hip to her toes, and she gasped.

Instantly Pa was at her side, his voice gentle. "Whoa there, young'un. Are you all right?"

"Yes, Pa. My leg just hurt all of the sudden. What's the surprise? Come on, please tell!" Her voice was shaky.

"All right. You close your eyes real tight, and I'll go get it. No peeking now!"

Obediently Alice closed her eyes tightly. She heard Pa's footsteps in the kitchen and then the mysterious bumps she'd heard before.

"*God Jul*, little one. Here's your surprise."

Again Pa stood in the doorway. In front of him was a kind of child's arm chair on wheels. It had a high back with a handle at the top, and the chair part sat raised up between four wheels like a wagon.

Below the chair a little platform stuck out like a shelf.

"What is it, Pa?" Alice asked. "Where'd you get it? Did Santa Claus bring it?"

"Nope, Santa Claus brought some other stuff, but I ordered this through the Sears and Roebuck catalog," Pa said. "It's called a go-cart. I looked at 'em in Rockford, but they were too expensive. I hear that city people use 'em to take little ones out in the fresh air when they can't walk good yet. Now you're not exactly a little one," he laughed, "but this'll help you get around. Want to try?"

"Yes! Please!" Alice said, holding up her arms. This time she clenched her jaw hard to keep from crying out at the pain in her leg. It hurt every time she was moved. But if she cried out, Pa would leave her in bed.

"There." He set her down and arranged her feet on the little shelf. "How about a ride?" He hurried behind the chair and pushed it through the door. "Gid-dap!" he called out.

"Look, Ma," Alice cried. "I'm getting around!" Ma stood near the sink with her hands clasped in front of her.

"Isn't that a nice surprise?" she said. "It's so

77

good to see you out of bed."

"Now how about those good Swedish pancakes you promised us, Mother?" Pa asked. "My belly is so empty it's turning inside out!" Just then Alice spotted her stocking propped against the back of a kitchen chair.

"Oh, Santa did come last night!" she cried. "Can I look in my stocking?"

"I think you can wait until after breakfast," Ma said. "We have to feed Pa before he fades away from hunger. Viola, you melt two tablespoons of lard for me in the frying pan."

Alice watched Ma begin to mix the batter for her delicious plate-sized Swedish pancakes. She cracked three eggs into the big yellow bowl and beat them with her whisk until they foamed and frothed. Then she added one and a half cups milk and stirred the egg-milk mixture vigorously.

She measured three-quarters cup flour, one-half teaspoon baking powder, one tablespoon sugar, and one-half teaspoon salt into her sifter. Then she turned the sifter handle, and the flour mixture fell like snow into the bowl. Quickly Ma stirred all the ingredients together.

"The lard is melted, Ma." Viola tilted the

78

Swedish Pancakes

2 Tbs. shortening
3 eggs
1 ½ cups milk
3/4 cup flour

½ tsp. baking powder
1 Tbs. sugar
½ tsp. salt

Melt shortening in 8" frying pan. Beat eggs in large bowl until frothy. Add milk and beat well. Add dry ingredients together in sifter and sift into egg mixture. Quickly stir together. Add melted shortening and stir.

Add small amount of shortening to pan. Spoon 3 Tbs. batter into pan and quickly tilt pan to cover bottom with batter. As soon as edges brown, flip to brown other side. Stack on warm platter while frying remainder of pancakes.

frying pan to make a pool of lard at the edge.

"Good. I'm just ready for it." Ma poured the lard into the batter and stirred again. "Now we're ready. You climb on your stool and get ready to grease the pans." With the point of a table knife Viola dropped a bit of lard in each of the two big skillets. Then Ma ladled three big spoons of batter into each. At once she tilted each pan until a paper-thin layer of batter covered the bottom. As soon as the edges began to brown and curl, Ma flipped the big thin pancake over to cook on the other side. When that side was speckled brown and cooked, she added the pancake to the stack on the old platter at the back of the cookstove. At last, with a stack more than four inches high, Ma brought the platter to the table. Alice's mouth watered, and she forgot about her stocking.

"Please fix mine first, Pa," she begged as he pushed her go-cart chair up to the table.

"You mean you don't want to fix your own?" Pa teased.

"No, you do it better. It comes in pieces when I try."

"All right, but we have to thank God for this good food before we do anythin'." They all bowed their heads, and Pa asked the blessing. Then Pa said, "Here goes."

He flipped two pancakes on a plate, popped on a pat of butter, and with a spoonful of lingonberries made an elegant figure eight on the top. Then he stuck his fork under the edge of the bottom pancake. With a flick of his wrist that was also a turn, he rolled the two pancakes together into a tight sausage-like roll, dripping butter and berry juice from the ends. He did it all with elegance and grace.

"Ummmmmmm." Alice bent over her plate with her mouth full. Pancakes and lingonberries made a breakfast worth waiting for.

"Ma, what're cranberries?" Viola's question broke into Alice's thoughts. "Our teacher said only cranberries grow in this country, not lingon-berries."

"She's right." When Ma answered, her voice sounded tired, and Alice looked up in surprise. "Lingonberries grow in Sweden, and they come here in big ships. But cranberries grow in the Wisconsin swamps. They're almost like lingonberries, only they're bigger and not so sweet. Maybe someday we won't be able to get lingonberries from Sweden. Then we'll have to eat cranberries on our pancakes."

81

She sighed and wiped her face with her hand-kerchief. "You know, Fred, I'm a little tired. I believe I'll go lay down for awhile. I must have got up too early this morning."

"You do that, Julia." Pa stood at once to pull back Ma's chair. "Viola and I can finish up here." His eyes twinkled. "And I'll see that the little one finishes up her breakfast before she digs into her stocking."

Ma was never tired or sick, and Alice felt anxious for a moment. But when Pa said "stocking" her thoughts of Ma disappeared at once.

"Hurry, Vi," she cried, and she licked the last bit of lingonberry juice from her fork. "Let's see what Santa put in our stockings!"

"I got to clear the table first," Vi said in her bossy way.

"But seein' as Ma's not here," Pa leaned forward to whisper, "we can put off the dishes for awhile. Put 'em to soak in the pan."

"Oh, hooray!" Viola bustled to stack the sticky plates in the dishpan, and she ladled hot water from the cookstove reservoir over them.

"Now, Pa?" Alice asked in a breathless voice.

"Yah, I guess so." Pa handed her the long-awaited stocking.

"One thing's nice about ugly long stockings," she thought. "There's lots of room for Christmas goodies." She dug into hers with both hands and pulled out—

"A new blue hair ribbon! Oooh, look Pa, I bet it matches my new dress." Then she burrowed further down and found a handkerchief with tatted lace. Next came a handful of nuts—walnuts, pecans, and hickory nuts. Underneath, at the very bottom of her stocking, was something round and big. It was pebbly, not smooth. She wiggled it out of the tight stocking, and she held it up triumphantly.

"It's an orange!" She rubbed her fingers over the pebbly skin and turned to her father. "How does Santa find oranges? They don't grow around here."

She still remembered the taste of an orange, for she'd had her first one last Christmas. The rubbery skin peeled away and inside was golden summery juice, each drop tied in its own tiny sack and all the sacks fastened together with white netting.

"That's right," Pa smiled. "Oranges grow in a place where it never snows. But Santa knows how to get there, and he brings 'em back for us at Christmas." He stopped and tugged on his moustache. "Now let me go see how Ma's feelin'. This is no day for her to spend in bed. This is a holiday."

Clutching her orange Alice watched Pa tiptoe to the front bedroom. She heard him say, "Are you all right, Julia?" Ma's answer came muffled.

"Course I'm all right. It's normal to be tired at a time like this."

But it wasn't normal for Ma—she never got tired. Alice looked down at her leg on the go-cart shelf. What did Ma mean when she said "at a time like this?" What was the matter with Ma?

Nine

Ma didn't stay in bed for long on Christmas Day. Soon she bustled around the kitchen—fixing Christmas dinner in her usual energetic way. But as the new year came, Alice noticed that her mother walked heavily. She often sat down with a big sigh, and she stayed in her rocking chair more than usual.

"What do you think's the matter with Ma?" Alice asked Viola one day. Vi thought a minute.

"She's getting old, I guess. And she's getting fat too. Anyhow," she added, "she's only tired and sick sometimes, so stop worrying!"

January was the very heart of winter—a cold and snowy month on Sandy Hollow Farm. Now that she had the go-cart, Alice was no longer forced to stay in bed all day. Each morning Ma helped her to dress and settled her into the go-cart seat. By pushing on the furniture and the door frames Alice was even able to move around a little by herself. But she was stuck in the house day after day, and she longed to be outside, to run and jump in the snow and especially to help Pa.

After Viola went off to school every morning, Pa went back outside to work with the colt he was training for the Rockford Fire Department. The horses that pulled the fire engines in the city were dapple-grays, the same as Nellie the buggy horse and Nellie's colt Star. So Pa was training Nellie's colt for a job as a fire horse. He spent hours in the paddock by the horse barn, teaching Star to stop and start and to turn on command. Sometimes Alice could hear him shouting, but she couldn't see him from any of the windows in the house.

Early one January afternoon Pa stuck his head in the kitchen door. "I'm off to that farm sale in New Milford, Julia," he said to Ma. "It don't look like it'll snow today, so I should be back before chore time easy." Ma sighed.

"I suppose you're looking for another horse. Seems to me like we have enough horses to feed

86

already."

"Now Mother," Pa said, and he laughed a little, "you know I only buy horses when they're a real bargain. Well—" he twirled his moustache and blew Alice a kiss, "I got to get goin'."

Alice pushed herself to the kitchen window and looked outside. She watched her father untie Nellie from the hitching post and rub her nose in a friendly way. Then he jumped in the little cutter, flapped the reins, and drove off—the cutter runners flying over the hard-packed snow.

"I wish I could go with him," she said to Ma. "I've never even been to a farm sale."

"It's mostly just machinery and animals so it wouldn't be much fun for you." Ma carried a jar of water into the sitting room and began to water the geraniums that grew in the sunny bay window. "I never cared much for them myself. But farm sales are your father's weakness. I bet he'll come home with another horse, and there'll be something wrong with it." Angrily she pinched off a withered red blossom. Alice stared at her mother in surprise.

"Why would Pa buy a horse that had something wrong with it?" she asked.

"Because he's a horse trader. He thinks it's

good business to buy a sad-looking horse that nobody else wants and then turn it into a good one. I have to admit that he's usually right, but we do move a lot of horses through this farm in a year." Ma looked out the window and sighed. "We'll just have to wait and

see what he brings home this time."

Alice sighed too, and suddenly Ma came back into the kitchen, and her voice was brisk.

"It's no matter. We can't sit around here wondering what your pa's going to do. How would

you like to help me bake cookies this afternoon? I haven't made cookies since before Christmas, and we don't have a one in the house."

"All right, Ma," Alice answered, "what kind shall we make?"

"I'll let you decide. Sugar cookies or *pepperkakor*?" Sugar cookies were the color of a pale yellow winter sun, and *pepperkakor* were dark spicy Swedish cookies.

"Let's make both!" Alice clapped her hands.

Ma laughed. "All right, but we have to make one kind at a time. You get out the cookie cutters, and I'll stir up the fire in the cookstove."

Ma mixed the sugar cookie dough first and rolled it out on the oil-cloth covered table. "Alice," she said, "you can cut out the shapes and put them in the pan. Keep them close together."

Alice sorted through the pile of cookie cutters. She chose a round sun shape and a crescent moon shape. Carefully she stamped each cutter into the soft dough.

"Grandpa will like these," she said. "He always likes your sugar cookies." Ma smiled as she slid a flat cookie pan into the oven.

"That's because my mother made this kind.

90

Sugar cookies have been Grandpa's favorite since I was a little girl." Alice rolled the bowl scrapings into little round balls of dough and flattened them on the cookie pan with a fork.

"What was it like when you were little, Ma?" She popped the last round ball of dough in her mouth.

"Life wasn't much different than it is now," Ma said. "I grew up right on this farm, you know. I was only three weeks old when we moved here. Grandpa and Grandma and Uncle Charley and I came all the way from Ishpeming."

"Ish—peming?"

"That's a town on a big lake up in Michigan. When we moved, Grandpa loaded our furniture in a big wagon and drove all the way here. Uncle Charley was a little boy, and I was a baby." The kitchen air was fragrant now. Alice took a deep breath of the good cookie smells and smiled at her mother.

"I thought Grandpa came from Sweden," she said. "Why did he buy this farm? Why didn't he stay in Ish—peming?" Ma checked the cookies in the oven and then poured herself a cup of coffee from the pot at the back of the cookstove.

"Grandpa and Grandma did come from Sweden,

91

honey, from a little village called Smebacken. Grandpa had worked in the Swedish iron mines, and when he came to America, he worked in the iron mines in Michigan. But times got bad, and there wasn't much work. So he decided to be a farmer. That was—let's see—in 1876."

Ma took a sip of coffee and continued. "And for a Swede, Rockford was a good place to move. So many Swedes live around here, it's almost like being in Sweden. Take Seventh Street for instance. All the stores and shops there are owned by Swedes, and everybody talks Swedish. If you remember when we go shopping, we always hear lots of people talking Swedish, and hardly anybody talks English."

"That's right, Ma," Alice said. "I never thought of that."

"In fact," Ma said, "did you know that Seventh Street is famous all over the world? I heard a story a few years ago about a man who lived on Seventh Street. He got a letter in the mail from Sweden. It was addressed to Mr. John A. Carlson, Seventh Street, USA. There was no city on the envelope at all, but the post office people knew about Seventh Street, and they knew they should send it to Rockford. Only thing was, there were nine different John A. Carlsons who lived on Seventh Street!" Ma laughed. "Now my little *Svenska flicka*, shall we start the *pepperkakor*? Viola should be here to help soon."

Ma was right. Alice was trying to stir the stiff brown *pepperkakor* dough without dumping it over the edge of the bowl when Vi burst into the kitchen. Her eyes sparkled, and her cheeks above her muffler glowed red from the cold wind.

"Wow! Is it ever cold out there! We had a snowball fight on the way home, and it was fun." She pulled off her mittens and shook them over Alice's head, showering snowflakes and tiny drops of water all over the table.

"And look, Ma! I got a red star! See, I got a red star on my arithmetic paper." She took a paper out of her lunch bucket and gave it to Ma. Ma studied the paper.

"That's real good, Viola. I'm proud of you for doing such good work. Why don't you show it to Alice?"

Behind Ma's back, Alice stuck out her tongue at her big sister. She hated not being able to go to school. Nobody gave *her* a red star for anything. And besides, Viola had barged in and spoiled the good time she was having with Ma.

93

"Dumb old red star!" she hollered.

"Why Alice, what a way to talk!" Ma's voice was sharp. "Shame on you. You should be happy for others when they do well. You go sit by yourself until you can be nice!"

Alice felt her lower lip trembling as she pushed herself to the window. "I won't cry!" she thought. "I'll show Vi I don't care." She stopped. "I'll watch for Pa. Will he really bring home a new horse? And what did Ma mean—a sad-looking horse?" She stared out at the driveway. Where was Pa anyhow?

The house was quiet, and the clock on the shelf ticked loudly. Soon the sun dropped behind the line of trees to the west, and the winter sky took on a dirty gray color. Alice watched anxiously for Pa. In the barn a cow bellowed.

"Isn't it time for Pa to come home?" she called to Ma.

"Yah, it's past time," Ma answered. "He's late, and it's time to do chores." She came to the doorway, pushing impatiently at a lock of hair from her topknot. "I hope he gets here soon. You can stay by the window and tell me if you see him coming."

Alice sighed and looked out the window again. It was too dark to see the road, but she could see the bare branches of the maples silhouetted black against the dark gray sky. She pressed an ear to the icy window—was that a horse's hoofs she heard?

"I think he's coming!" she called.

"Does he have a horse in back of the cutter?" Ma asked.

Alice breathed on the cold glass and wiped the frost away to make a clear spot. She strained her eyes. Yes, here came Nell, turning off Sandy Hollow Road, but going very slowly, almost walking. And yes, a new horse was tied to the cutter. The strange group slowly passed by the window—clop, clop, LIMP—clop, clop, LIMP—clop, clop, LIMP.

"Ma!" Alice's words came in a gasp. "That horse behind the cutter, he's limping terrible! Pa didn't buy a sad-looking horse, he bought a sick-looking horse! Oh, the poor thing!"

Ten

It was pitch black outside, and the cows were bellowing to be milked before Pa had Nell and the sick-looking horse unhitched and stabled. Alice kept her nose pressed to the glass of the kitchen window until she saw a flare of light in the barn.

"Pa's in the cowbarn. I can see the lantern," she said to her mother. "Will he come in and tell us what's wrong with that new horse?" Ma was making stew, and she stirred the bubbling pot before she answered.

"No, he has to finish all the chores before he comes in." She looked at Alice. "You're getting around so well I believe you can help Viola with supper. That way I can go out and help with the milking." Alice's heart thumped so loud she thought Ma could hear.

"Sure, Ma, I can do that. We can get along fine without you."

It was true that Alice had learned to get around handily in her go-cart. She'd learned how to push it to go through doors and around corners, and she'd found that she could even carry things from one room to another by putting them on her lap. Her leg still ached most of the time, but so long as she didn't try to put any weight on it or use it in any way, she was able to tolerate the pain. As she helped set the table for supper that night, she began to plan.

"Vi," she asked, "when's the new term start at school?"

Viola set the butter dish on the table. "Two weeks," she answered. "We're just finishing up our lessons now. I bet Minnie won't be promoted a grade like she should be though. She doesn't know her arithmetic at all. What do you want to know for?"

"Just wondering," Alice answered. She was getting older all the time. She was supposed to be in school this year, and she would be except for that useless leg. Still—if she could get around in the schoolroom in her go-cart like she got around in the house, maybe Ma and Pa would let her go to school to start with the new term. All she had to prove was that she could manage things by herself.

"I'll do all kinds of things to help Ma," she thought to herself. "She'll see how well I can manage. I could even help Pa with that sick-looking horse if he'd let me out in the barn!"

As soon as Pa came in for supper that night, Alice asked about the sick-looking horse. Pa raised his eyebrows.

"Don't you worry about that new horse. Gypsy's been neglected, and she's got an infected hoof and a sore leg. But I can fix her up good as new. You'll see."

"What do you have to do, Pa?" Alice asked.

"Why I have to fix her infected hoof and rub the muscles in her sore leg with that good green horse liniment. Then she needs to be fattened up, and she'll need new shoes." He shook his head. "I don't see how some farmers think they can get any work out of a horse if they don't treat 'em right. But I bought her for a good price because that farmer didn't want to feed her all winter with her bad leg an' all." He turned to Viola.

"You'll be home from school tomorrow. How'd

98

you like to come out and help me? You might's well learn how to take care of a lame horse."

Viola shuddered. "If that horse is sick, I'm staying in here. I don't want to mess with a sick horse."

"Squeamish, huh?" Pa tugged on a moustache end. "Guess I'll have to do it myself then."

"Pa," Alice broke in impatiently, "can't I come out and help? You see how well I can get around in the go-cart."

Pa shook his head. "No, little one, it's too hard to push you through the snow in the barnyard. I'm afraid you'll have to stay in the house. You help Ma with her chores in here."

Alice clenched her teeth. She *had* to be able to start the new term at school. How could she convince Pa?

As soon as Ma pushed her go-cart into the steamy kitchen the next morning, Alice knew it was wash day. A giant copper wash boiler almost covered the top of the cookstove and sent curl after curl of steam into the warm air.

"Busy day today," Ma said, "so breakfast will be simple—just bread and milk and fried potatoes." She looked out the window where the cold morning

99

light was seeping into the blackness. "Wonder if it'll snow today. I'd sure like to hang the clothes outside because they dry so much faster. Think I'll chance it."

"I'll help, Ma," Alice said.

Ma looked surprised for a minute, then nodded. "Of course. You can wipe dishes for Viola after breakfast and stack them on the counter. That'll be a big help." She brushed her hand lightly over Alice's hair. "Now I got to get busy or that wash will never get done."

After breakfast she opened the door to the glassed-in entry porch, and cold air swooped into the kitchen. Alice shivered and pulled herself closer to the cookstove.

In a minute Ma returned walking backward and pulling the washing machine into the kitchen. The washing machine was a big wooden tub on legs. Inside was a slanted cradle with a handle. By pushing the handle back and forth Ma could agitate the clothes and loosen the dirt. She left the washing machine in the middle of the kitchen near the cistern pump and hurried back to the porch. This time she carried in two big galvanized tubs and set them on the long counter.

101

"Brrr. It's cold out there," she said, slamming the door behind her. "I'll freeze my fingers hanging out the clothes, that's for sure." She tested the steaming water in the wash boiler. "Almost boiling. That'll give me time to strip the beds and sort the clothes. Viola, after you finish the dishes, you can make up the beds and then straighten the house." Viola turned from the dishpan.

"All that by myself?" she asked in a whiny way.

Ma stopped, and her brown eyes flashed angrily. "Yes, all that. Let's hear no more complaining. There's plenty of work to do! You get the soap and the bluing out of the cupboard for me, will you Alice?"

She disappeared with a swish of skirts, and Alice pushed herself to the cupboard where Ma kept the starch, the bluing, and a jar of shavings from hard yellow bar soap.

Bluing was a dark indigo blue liquid almost like ink, and the dried part around the top stained her fingers in blue streaks when she shook the bottle. She liked to watch the blue bubbles inside break and disappear as the liquid settled out. Ma always added a few drops of bluing to the last rinse water. "It keeps white clothes from turning yellow," she said, "especially in the winter when there's no sun to bleach them out."

Alice shook the bottle once more, but her sister clattered two plates together. "Stop playing with the bluing, Al, and come wipe the dishes," she said. "You're getting behind." Just then Ma appeared in the doorway, her face almost hidden by the big bundle of dirty clothes in her arms.

"Oooof!" Ma said. "I can hardly get through the door. I'll be glad when you're well enough so you and Viola can share the bed again. Then I won't have so many sheets to wash." She dropped her bundle on the floor and began sorting the dirty clothes into piles by color.

Pa's white shirts for church and other white clothes that would be boiled were washed first. Then came underwear and the heavy muslin sheets. The next pile Ma called "light colored clothes." It included the girls' everyday dresses and Ma's aprons and dresses. Then came a big pile of dark work clothes, and last of all, the rag rugs. Ma washed each of these piles in order from white to dark. She used the hottest water for the white things, and when they were clean, she took them out and put in the colored clothes.

"At last we're ready to wash!" Ma straightened up and put a hand to her back. "Shake some of those soap shavings into the machine, will you honey?"

Alice hung her dishtowel on a hook and pushed herself to the washing machine. She unscrewed the lid of the jar and dipped her hand into the squiggles of yellow soap, dropping them into the wooden tub. Ma added steaming water from the copper wash boiler on the stove, and the soap began to melt and run together.

All morning Ma moved between cookstove and washtub, with Alice helping as much as she could. Viola was still cross, and she stomped through the rest of the house, making beds and putting things away. But she stayed away from the kitchen.

Ma boiled the white clothes, scrubbed the dirty spots on the tinny ridged washboard, and added bluing to the rinse water. When the clothes were clean, she lifted the dripping material to feed it through the wringer while Alice turned the crank as fast as she could. The clothes rippled from the wringer like ribbon candy and fell in neat folds into the wash basket.

In the summer Ma washed on the glassed-in porch where it was cooler, and winter or summer she

104

hung the clothes outside whenever she could. On windy summer days the sheets crackled and boomed like whips, drying soft and smooth in an hour. But now that it was winter it took all day before the heaviest of the clothes dried. First they froze—hard and wrinkly like *lutefisk*. Then the clothes dried, but everything stayed stiff and boardy till it was shaken out and folded or sprinkled for the ironing basket. From the doorway of the sitting room Alice watched her mother struggle with the heavy wet sheets.

"Now I know why you only wash one sheet from my bed every week, Ma," she said. "It's because they're so big and heavy."

"That's right, honey. Some people don't even wash that often. But I rotate the sheets every week. I put the top sheet on the bottom and wash the bottom sheet, and they stay pretty clean. You have to wash your feet before you go to bed, though, 'specially in summer when you run barefoot." Suddenly Ma stopped talking, and she turned with a wide-eyed look.

The words "running barefoot" stabbed like a knife. Alice sat very still in her go-cart, looking down at her lap. Then big tears brimmed over and ran down her cheeks. Ma left her washing and knelt

105

beside the go-cart, her arms dripping wet.

"Honey, I'm sorry," she said with a catch in her voice. "I just wasn't thinking. But someday you'll run barefoot again. I'm sure of it." She lifted the corner of her apron and wiped away the tears.

Ma's slip of the tongue made Alice more determined than ever to show that she could manage by herself. Toward the end of the day she could see that her mother was getting tired. Once Ma even sat down in her kitchen rocker panting from climbing the steps.

"She really needs me to help her," Alice thought. "Vi doesn't even care how tired she is." Just then Ma pushed herself to her feet again.

"Now for the last load," she said. She went to the sitting room door and raised her voice. "Viola," she called, "I want you to go outside and see if those shirts are dry yet. If they are, take them in because I need more space on the line."

Viola answered from the front of the house. "In a minute, Ma. I have to get my coat."

Ma went back to the washer and pushed the handle a few more times. Then she lifted the heavy work clothes to feed them through the wringer. "Alice, you've been a big help today," she said. "I don't know what I'd have done without you. Now when I get these hung up, all I have to do is empty the water and clean up the kitchen." She grunted softly as she hoisted the heavy wash basket and headed for the door.

As soon as she went outside, Alice moved quickly. She put the soap chips and the bluing away in the cupboard, and she tidied up the kitchen as well as she could. Then she eyed the big wooden washer. She knew Ma had to dump the water outside, and the wooden tub was heavy. How could she help?

"I know," she said to herself. "If I get my go-cart backwards, I can push with my good leg and pull the washer after me to the door. Then all Ma will have to do is carry the water down the steps. She'll be glad I saved her so much work. And I bet she'll let me go to school then too."

Carefully she turned around in the go-cart and lined it up with the door to the entry porch. She lifted her good leg off the little shelf and planted it firmly on the floor. Then she grabbed the wooden washer with both hands and began to pull it after her.

At first the washer stayed right where it was no matter how Alice tugged and pulled. But finally it began to move on the wet floor boards—slowly, slowly. Alice felt her heart pounding hard in her chest, and her left leg twitched and strained. But she was doing it!

She got to the kitchen door and twisted around in her chair to turn the doorknob. Then she backed slowly through the door, still pushing with her foot and pulling the washer after her. But on the doorsill the washer stuck fast. What could she do? She tugged and tugged. Tears came to her eyes, and she gave a mighty push with her foot.

Suddenly her hands slipped off the soapy wooden edge of the washer tub. The washer rocked back and forth, and some of the water slopped over the side. Worse still, Alice felt herself shooting across the floor of the glassed-in entry porch—backwards toward the outside door.

She reached out to grab at anything, but since she was through the doorway, there was nothing she could reach. She felt the back wheels of the go-cart touch the outside door, and the door—unlatched— began to swing open.

"Pa!" She screamed the word out, clutching the frame of the door with both hands. The icy outside air seared her lungs, but she screamed again. "Pa!" At last she heard heavy footsteps pounding up the path shoveled in the snow.

"Alice! What the . . . ?" Then his hands were on the back of the go-cart, and she could let go.

"Oh Pa!" She sobbed in relief as he pushed her back into the entry porch.

"What happened?" he asked. Then he saw the washer in the middle of the doorsill, the water still sloshing from side to side. He cupped her chin in one big hand. "You were tryin' to help your Ma, weren't you?"

As he spoke, Ma herself rushed up the steps, Viola right behind her. "What's wrong, Fred? Alice, what happened? What made you scream?"

"What're you doing out here, Al?" Viola asked.

Pa turned and shook his head at both of them. "It's all right. Alice slipped a little in the go-cart. I'll take care o' this if you got more clothes to hang up."

Alice looked from Pa to Ma and back to Pa. Something in Pa's eyes spoke to Ma, for she pulled her coat around her shoulders with one hand and turned away. "Come along, Viola. Let's finish hanging up those work clothes."

Pa lifted the wooden washer out of the doorway and set it back inside the kitchen. Then he pushed

GOD'S GREEN LINIMENT

Alice's go-cart over the sill. He sat down on a kitchen
chair and took both Alice's trembling hands in his.

"Now tell me," he said.

"Pa, I *got* to go to school!" Alice gulped. He
nodded, but he didn't say anything.

"And I can get around real good in my go-cart
now, so I thought even if I can't walk . . . " Pa's
eyes were a very deep blue, and they seemed to look
right inside her.

". . . I thought if I could show you how much I
could do in my go-cart, you'd let me go to school,
and maybe even help in the barn a little when the
snow is gone."

Pa sighed. "Alice, Alice. I got to admire your
spunk. But you can see what can happen when you
try to do more than you can manage." He tightened
his grip on her hands.

"I'm afraid you can't go to school this year
unless you can walk. I already talked to the other
school board members, and they think it would be
too much to ask of the teacher. And I'd have to take
you there every day, and I can't always get away."

"And Alice," Pa was very serious now, "I can't
have you takin' chances like you did just now. What
if I hadn't been right there at the milkhouse to catch

110

you?   You know Ma's feelin' poorly, and in her condition she wouldn't have been able to keep you from fallin' down those steps in the go-cart.''

"But Pa, I only wanted to help!"

"I know, little one, I know. But your way isn't the way to do it. You got to keep prayin' and believin' that God will heal you. You got to ask for a miracle." Pa turned away and pulled his handkerchief out of his pocket. "Maybe by next year things'll work out." He blew his nose with a big honk.

Alice dropped her eyes to her lap. There seemed to be no way to get to school. —But there had to be!

Eleven

A thaw set in during the last week of January. After a few days the snowdrifts along Sandy Hollow Road hunched themselves smaller, and a trickle of water ran down the driveway. A few patches of brown mud began to show through the mushy snow in the wagon yard.

"Is it almost spring, Pa?" Alice asked as she looked out the sitting room window.

"Nope, afraid it's a long time till spring, little one. This is just a warm spell, and it'll probably snow again in a few days." Then Pa smiled. "Maybe tomorrow though we can find out for sure."

"Find out what? What do you mean?"

"Tomorrow's February 2, and that's Ground

Hog Day. The story is that if Mr. Ground Hog peeps
out o' his hole on February 2 and sees his shadow,
there'll be six more weeks of winter. But if there's
no shadow, spring will soon be here."

"But Pa," Alice asked with a worried frown,
"what's a ground hog? Our hogs don't sleep in holes
in the ground!"

Pa didn't laugh at her question. He only smiled.
"Course they don't. The ground hog is a furry little
fella that lives in the banks along the fields or by the
creek. He looks sort of like a squirrel, but he don't
have a big bushy tail. Out in the east I guess people
call 'em wood chucks."

"Wood chucks? That's a funny name."

"Yah, they have two funny names, ground hog
and wood chuck. But they're not hogs or chucks—
they're little shy creatures of their own kind. They
eat our oats and our hay, but they don't do much
damage. Don't see too many of 'em around here, but
I did see a burrow at the edge of the field back of the
barn. Might be one there."

"Oh, what fun! But how can we find out?"
Alice looked down at her useless leg.

Pa's answer was cheerful. "Wait till tomorrow,
little one, and we'll see what we can see."

GOD'S GREEN LINIMENT

February 2 was a Tuesday, and the day promised to be warm and sunny. After breakfast Viola sat on a high-backed kitchen chair and pulled on her buckle galoshes.

"I don't need mittens today, Ma," she said. "It's like spring outside." Ma answered from the bay window in the sitting room.

"Keep your mittens in your pocket anyhow. You never know what it'll be like by the end of the day. And hurry, my dear, you're late."

"Oh, late, late. I don't even want to go to school!" Viola muttered the words, too softly for Ma to hear.

But Alice, who sat in her go-cart by the cistern pump, heard everything Vi said, and she couldn't believe her ears.

"What do you mean, you don't want to go to school?" She stared at her sister. The new term had started, and she'd hoped more than anything to be on her way to school herself. Viola looked up.

"Well, school's hard work, you know. Be glad all you have to do is stay home and play." She snapped the last buckle on her galoshes and picked up her lunch pail.

"Bye Ma!" she called.

114

But there was no answer.

"That's funny. Ma must've gone in her bedroom. Oh, well, see you later." She pushed open the door and hurried down the steps.

Alice stuck out her tongue at her sister as the door banged shut. "It's not fair!" she said. Then, suddenly, she was worried. It wasn't like Ma not to say goodby to Viola. Was she sick again? She pushed herself into the sitting room.

"Ma? Ma? Where are you?"

To her surprise, Ma was sitting right there in her rocking chair, but she had a strange look on her face.

"Ma, are you all right?"

"Yah, I'm all right," Ma answered. "I just had a stitch in my side. Did you see Viola off?"

Alice nodded.

"Then how about if you call Pa for me," Ma went on. "Ask him if he'll step in here a minute. I think he's in the milkhouse so he can hear you from the kitchen."

Reassured by Ma's everyday voice, Alice pushed herself back to the kitchen. She tugged at the window until it lifted and called her father. In a minute she heard the milkhouse door slam, and he headed across the wagon yard toward the house.

"Brought Ma some nice fresh eggs," he said, bringing a pail into the kitchen. He looked into the sitting room and raised his eyebrows. "Alice, take these eggs out o' the pail for me, will you? You can put 'em in Ma's egg bowl."

Alice was carefully fitting the last of the pearly eggs into the big egg bowl when Pa came back into the kitchen. He was whistling. He tugged on Alice's braid as he passed her go-cart.

"It's a warm day today, and there's not much snow in the barnyard," he said. "How'd you like to go out to the barn with me, little one?" Alice's heart skipped a beat, and she nearly dropped the last egg.

"Oh Pa, can I really?"

"Don't see why not. We'll put your coat on, and your muffler. I got to spend some time workin' on Gypsy's sore leg, and I recollect that you wanted to see her up close." He winked elaborately and reached into the cupboard for the big bottle of green horse liniment.

A few minutes later Alice found herself outside for the first time in many months. She took deep breaths of the spring-like air as Pa bumped her go-cart across the gravelly wagon yard.

116

"Good thing it ain't any warmer than it is," he laughed. "Otherwise you'd be stuck in the mud, young lady." He pushed the sliding door of the horsebarn open with his elbow and lifted the front of the go-cart over the edge. Nell looked up from her manger to nicker a welcome.

"Oh Nellie, you do remember me, don't you!" Alice felt like crying she was so happy. "Pa, it even *smells* good here in the barn." Pa pushed her go-cart across the wide boards to Nellie's stall and parked it there.

"You can give Nell a rub on the nose for a minute," he said. "I got to go back to the house and get the liniment and some rags."

Nellie poked her head out between the bars of her stall and nibbled at Alice's fingertips.

"I bet you're looking for a carrot, aren't you? And I don't have one today. But next time I promise I'll bring one." She rubbed her fingers on Nell's velvety nose—a funny gray velvet with stiff prickly hairs poking out.

Alice loved all the horses on Sandy Hollow Farm, but Nell was her special favorite. Her legs were long and sleek, and her dapple gray coat shone in the sunlight. Blackie and Prince, Pa's team of workhorses, were much bigger and stronger than Nell, but Nell had a spark of wild spirit that they lacked.

"She's really a buggy horse," Pa had said, "and she's proud when she's trotting along to church on a Sunday morning. Still she helps us out in the spring and summer whenever we need a hand, and she works right along with Blackie and Prince for the heavy stuff like plowin'."

Now Nell nickered again, and from across the barn her colt Star answered her. Gypsy, the new horse, moved restlessly in her box stall in the corner. Alice sighed happily. How good it was to be back in the barn! But where was Pa? He seemed to be taking a long time.

Just then she heard Pa's whistle. He pushed the barn door open, stomping the mud off his feet. In his hand he carried the big bottle of green liniment and a worn muslin sheet.

"Push yourself over to the box stall, Alice," he said. "That way you can keep me company and watch what I'm doin'." He lifted the latch and went into the box stall, speaking softly to the new horse.

"Reach me the hoof pick off the nail," he said as he unwrapped a long strip of bandage from Gypsy's leg. "I got to keep her hoofs cleaned out good. When

I bought her, a small stone had lodged in one, and it worked around and started an infection. That started her limpin', and then her muscles got stiff. Besides, her hoofs haven't been trimmed since last year sometime." He shook his head. "No wonder you limp, Gypsy girl."

Alice handed Pa the hoof pick, a curved piece of metal about six inches long with a sharpened hook on one end. He lifted the horse's front leg and leaned

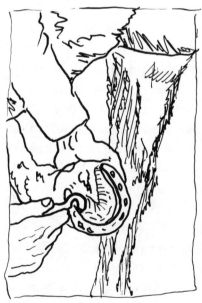

it against his knee. Gypsy shuddered, but Pa spoke reassuringly.

"Take it easy, old girl. You're gettin' better, and we'll have you fixed up good as new 'fore you know it." As he talked, Pa carefully cleaned out an accumulation of dirt and packed manure from the hoof.

119

"How did you know she was a good horse to buy at the farm sale?" Alice asked. "How can you tell?"

Pa chuckled. "I been around horses since I was a boy," he said. "When I was in the Swedish army, I learned what to look for in a horse. I make sure to get to a farm sale early, and I check out the horses first thing. I watch 'em walk, and I look at their teeth to see how old they are. Then I feel their legs and look at each hoof." He set down one hoof and lifted another.

"You can find out lots about a horse if you look careful," he continued, "and you don't want to believe everything the owner tells you. Hmm." He looked down at the hoof he was cleaning. "It's healin' just fine. She had a corn from that stone that was wedged in her foot. It'd bruised the tender part of her hoof. But I cut it out, and it's gettin' better." He set the hoof down.

Alice watched Pa's hands. "Does that mean she's well?"

"Not yet," Pa answered, "but she's gettin' there. Now I just got to keep rubbin' her sore leg with liniment and keep it wrapped up. Hand me the liniment bottle."

GOD'S GREEN LINIMENT

He opened the big bottle and tilted a pool of green liquid into his hand. At once the horse barn was filled with the strong green smell—a stingy and nose-puckering smell that seemed to sink right through the skin. Pa looked up and laughed at Alice's wrinkled up nose.

"Why, I think this stuff smells good!" he said. Now he began rubbing Gypsy's leg—up and down, up and down, with long sure strokes. Alice took a deep breath.

"How come you rub her leg that way? What's that do?" Pa's hands moved up and down as he answered.

"One problem all horses have is poor circulation. That means it's hard for the blood to move all the way down their long legs. So when they have a sore, it takes a long time to heal. And sometimes when they limp, their muscles get stiff from favoring one leg."

He added more liniment and continued. "When I rub 'em like this, it warms the skin and makes the blood move. Then they heal faster."

"You mean . . . that's all you have to do?"

Pa laughed. "Well, o' course it takes time. One or two rubbings won't do it, 'cause all the muscles

121

have to heal and get strong again. But if I keep rubbin' everyday, by the time spring comes I'm sure Gypsy'll be runnin' without any limp at all."

Gypsy blew out a sigh through her lips, and in the next stall Nell poked her nose through the slats and nickered anxiously. Pa turned to Alice with a smile.

"You better go give Nellie some attention. I believe she's gettin' jealous!"

Alice pushed herself back to Nellie, her go-cart bumping over the uneven floor. In a minute Pa capped the liniment bottle and wiped his hands on the old sheet.

"That'll do for awhile," he said. "D'you still remember what day it is, little one?"

"Oh yes, Pa," Alice smiled, "it's Ground Hog Day. Can we go look for Mr. Ground Hog?" Pa's eyes crinkled in the corners.

"Thought we might take a look around the back field. It's too muddy out there for a go-cart though, so you'll have to ride on my shoulders. D'you think you can manage that?" Alice felt a twinge of fear because she knew her leg would hurt more than ever dangling down like that. But on her first day outside, she would not admit that to her father.

122

"Sure, Pa," she said, "My leg is much better."
Pa came out of Gypsy's stall and carefully latched the
gate.

"I'll push you over to the corn crib first," he
said, "and we'll leave the go-cart there."

As soon as they were outside the horse barn,
Alice noticed a strange buggy tied up at the hitching
post by the back door. She felt the go-cart jerk as Pa
quickened his pace.

"Look, Pa," she said, "somebody's come to
visit."

"Why so they have. Might be a horse buyer
come from Rockford to look at Nell's colt. Let's
see—" the go-cart stopped a minute midway between
the corn crib and the barn. "Tell you what, little
one," Pa finally said, "I'll take you to the corn crib
and you can run the fan mill for me while I step in
the house and see who it is. It'll be just like old times
with you helpin' me."

Alice felt a glow of pleasure. Pa hadn't forgotten
her disappointment at not being able to start the new
term of school, and he was letting her help. But it
did seem early in the year to be getting seed ready for
planting.

The corn crib smelled good too—a different

smell from the one in the horse barn. The walls were lined with big bins that held the dried corn cobs and the kernels of oats, barley, and wheat. The smell was dry and clean and smooth. The center was an open space where Pa could drive a wagon right through in the summer time. Now, though, the center was full of farm machinery, cleaned and well-oiled and parked out of the snow until summer. High above Alice's head she could see more machinery that Pa had hoisted on ropes and hung from the rafters out of the way.

Pa seemed to be in a big hurry. He pushed Alice up to the fan mill and went to get a pail of oats. The fan mill was a box-like machine about as big as Ma's china closet with a crank on the side. When the crank was turned, several screens shook back and forth and sifted the weed seeds and chaff from the good oat seeds. It took a long time to sift all the grain for planting. Pa poured the oats in the chute of the fan mill.

"There you go, little one," he said. "It'll be a big help if you start on the seed oats for me." He set the pail down and stepped quickly out the door.

Alice pulled the handle down with both hands and began to turn it round and round. It was hard to do from a sitting position, and she wished for the hundredth time that she could stand up. What if she had to spend her whole life sitting down? She pushed the ugly thought out of her mind.

Then she thought about ground hogs—little furry creatures that Pa said lived in burrows underground. She tried to think how an underground house would look. Would it be like the cellar, damp and mysteriously dark and full of spiders? All the time she was thinking, she cranked the fan mill handle round and round. The screens clattered back and forth, and a small cloud of fine chaff rose in the air. It reminded her of threshing day and the big iron beetle. She shuddered. Suddenly—

Clang! Clang!

"That's the dinner bell," she thought. "Why's the dinner bell ringing? Ma only rings it to call Pa when he's in the fields, or when something's wrong." She swallowed hard and listened again. "What's wrong? Did something happen to Ma?"

Twelve

CLANG! CLANG! The corn crib door was open only a crack, but the dinner bell was loud and urgent. Her heart pounding, Alice pushed herself away from the fan mill. The clanging bell made her want to run, and tears of anger came into her eyes and ran down her cheeks as she struggled to get to the door. With a mighty shove she pushed the crack wider.

Then she saw Pa. He was ringing and ringing and clanging the dinner bell—all the time dancing a kind of bumpy jig on the porch steps.

"Pa, what is it?" Alice shrieked the words across the wagon yard.

Pa let go the bell rope and bounded across the

126

slush, his boots spraying mud with each step. She looked at him as he ran. He didn't look worried. In fact, his face was split in two by the size of his smile, and the points of his moustache quivered.

At the door he caught her up in a big hug. "It's a present for you!" he shouted. "You got a new baby brother!"

He whirled her around once, forgetting her leg, and then set her down on the go-cart seat. "A baby!" she thought, and her heart pounded. "Somebody who's littler than me!" She looked up at her father.

"You mean—we got a baby of our own?"

Pa laughed his big booming laugh. "I'll say. And he's a big one! Want to go see, little one?" He rolled the door shut and started the go-cart down the slant to the wagon yard. At the house he carried her—muddy go-cart and all—up the steps and into the entry porch. He set her down with a thump and turned to shut the door. Alice pulled the kitchen door open.

"Ma! Ma!" she called, "where's the . . . " She stopped and stared. A strange man stood at the sink, pumping water from the cistern into a wash pan. His coat was off, and his shirt sleeves were rolled to his elbows. The stranger turned as she opened the door,

127

and he looked over the top of his spectacles. It was Dr. Banks.

"Hello, young lady," he said in his deep voice, "coming to see your new brother? He's a fine big baby!"

"So that's where the strange buggy came from," she thought. Pa must have called him on the telephone. But the doctor—did that mean Ma was really sick? She tugged at Pa's hand.

"Where's Ma?" she asked. "Please, can I go see Ma?"

"Sure you can go see her," he answered. "Come along to the bedroom. Only maybe I better wipe the mud off your go-cart wheels first."

A minute later Alice peeked around the door frame of Ma and Pa's bedroom, almost afraid to look. Ma had been sickly off and on for so long, and now the doctor was here . . . but then she saw Ma's rosy and smiling face.

"Ma! Oh, Ma," she said. Behind her Pa gave the go-cart a push, and her mother reached out with one arm to hug her. "Are you all right, Ma?"

"Why honey, don't cry. I'm fine, couldn't be better. I'm just resting. And look—here's our new baby!" Nestled in the crook of her mother's other

128

arm was a red and wrinkled baby. His eyes were tightly shut and his face wore a scowl.

Alice stared. "But he's all red!" she cried. "And he's so little. Pa said we had a big baby, but he's too little to play with me!" Her voice quivered with disappointment, but Ma paid no attention.

"He'll grow," she said. "Someday he'll be bigger than you, I expect." From the doorway behind her Pa cleared his throat.

"Want to hear his name? It's Lawrence Charles Lindstrom—and we'll call him Larry." He came in the room and knelt beside Alice, peering at the baby. "Ain't he somethin'?"

In all the excitement Alice had forgotten about the ground hog. Now she remembered, and she touched her father's shoulder.

"Oh Pa, we never did go to look at the ground hog hole. How'll we know when spring will come?" Pa stood up to look out the window.

"We got a little busy to do that, didn't we? Hmmm. The sun's still shining, even through those thin clouds in the sky." He turned as the doctor came into the room. "What do you think, Dr. Banks? Would a ground hog see his shadow on a day like this?"

129

"A ground hog?" The doctor pursed his lips. "Yes, I would say he would. I'm afraid we're in for six more weeks of winter. And I'm ready for spring." He sighed and bent over the baby. Then he patted Ma's shoulder. "Everything seems fine here, and I understand a neighbor is coming in to help. Let me know if you need me again."

Then he turned to Pa. "While I'm here, suppose I take a look at your little girl's leg. I haven't examined her for quite some time." He looked down at the go-cart with a frown. "I see you've let her get out of bed. She was supposed to keep that leg absolutely still to rest it."

Alice looked up at Pa anxiously, and even he looked worried. "It didn't seem right to keep her in bed when she started feelin' better," he said. He cleared his throat. "I'll take her into the sitting room and put her on the sofa so you can look at her leg."

Lying on her back on the sofa Alice stared at the shelf over her head. She listened to the ticking clock and tried not to watch the doctor. He listened to her heart and poked and probed her body. He pulled the long stocking off her good leg. Then she knew, though she could not feel it, that he had pulled the long stocking off the bad leg, and he was

130

examining it. She heard him sigh.

"What is it?" Ma called from the bedroom. "How does it look?"

Slowly the doctor walked away—back into Ma's bedroom. Slowly Pa followed him. Their voices were hushed and the words muffled, but Alice propped herself up on her elbows and strained to hear.

"She seems healthy enough," Dr. Banks said. "Her color is good, and her heart is strong. And the leg hasn't twisted even though you've let her get out of bed."

"—and how is her leg?" Pa's voice rumbled in his chest.

"—following the usual pattern in cases like this. I'm afraid the muscles are wasting away. She seems to have no more sensation than she did in the beginning, and the muscles are definitely weakening. I looked at both legs, and the afflicted one appears to be quite a bit shorter. I'm sorry, but she'll probably never walk again."

Alice stopped breathing and stared down at her legs. The good leg twitched, and she crooked it at the knee. But the bad leg was pale and thin, and it lay there like a dead thing. The doctor's cruel voice went on.

131

"It's a shame, but you should be grateful that now you have a fine sturdy boy. He's a big strong baby, and he'll make a good farmer some day. —Well, I must be going on."

Alice gulped, and fear clamped her throat tight shut. Today she'd been out helping Pa, and it had been almost like old times. She had begun to hope again—to even hope that she might walk.

But with the doctor's words, her hopes died. She had tried to walk, and she had failed. She had tried to prove her independence in the go-cart so she could go to school, and she had failed. Now would this new baby take her place as Pa's helper? If she could never walk, Pa wouldn't need her in the barn anymore, would he? She turned her face to the wall as the doctor and Pa walked through the sitting room. And somewhere in the middle of her fear she began to hate the new baby who was taking her place.

Thirteen

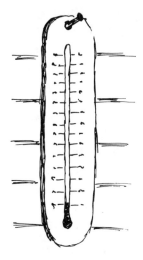

After the February thaw on Ground Hog Day, winter came back to Sandy Hollow Farm. The red liquid in the thermometer outside the kitchen window dropped way down and stayed there. Fierce winds blew out of the north bringing snow—buffeting the farm house and rattling the shutters. The cold dry snow piled up outside the foundation, even sifting between the cracks and into the house. All through February and into March the winds brought snow.

The new baby slept and ate, gurgled and grew. All Ma's extra time was taken up with rocking him or feeding him. Alice held him sometimes and watched him often, but in her heart the small flame of hatred kept burning. She could hear the doctor's words.

". . . afraid she'll never walk again. But be glad you got this new baby . . . . He'll make a good farmer someday."

She listened to Ma and Pa praying, but their

133

words had lost all meaning. At Christmas she had believed Pa when he had told her she needed patience, and she had been patient, but for nothing. Except for that small flame of hatred Alice was as frozen inside as one of the big icicles that hung from the eaves.

Then spring came to Sandy Hollow Farm.

For weeks the cold wind had blown from the north with the sharpness of winter. But one day the wind shifted to the south, then picked up speed and whistled around corners, blowing hard for two days. By the third day the wind died down, and the air grew warmer. Along the rise toward the river white clouds massed and began to tower higher and higher. The fourth morning it rained—a spring rain, warm to the touch, Ma said, and soft to the skin. Winter had blown away.

The next Sunday Viola jumped down from the buggy and raced into the house before Nellie had properly stopped.

"Ma! Ma! I got a piece to say in the Easter program!" The words tumbled out excitedly, and she plunged her hand into her pocket and pulled out a scrap of paper. "See! Our teacher gave us each a piece to say all by ourselves!" Ma was rocking the baby by the sunny bay window.

"How nice," she said. "I'm sure you'll do it very well. And it'll be a good chance to practice your Swedish." She pushed her spectacles down her nose and reached for the paper. "Let me see what it says." She held up the paper and read:

> *"Jesu Kristui uppstod från de döda i dag*
> *En ängel sade 'Kom och se*
> *Han är icke här,*
> *Ve behöver inte frukta längre.' "*

Alice sat quietly in her go-cart by the dining room table and listened. All Sunday morning she'd been idly turning the pages of an old picture book. She wanted to go to Sunday School even if she had to go in the go-cart, but Pa had said she must wait until the weather was warmer. "Then Ma will be able to go to church too," he'd said. "But now the baby is too little."

—Always the baby.

Now she listened to the words of Vi's piece as Ma read them from the paper, and she thought how they would sound in English. She whispered the words to herself.

> "Jesus Christ rose today
> And God had an angel say,

135

'Come and see. He is not here.
You no longer need to fear.' "
"It's an easy piece," she said to herself. "I could say that."

But she couldn't. She'd never be able to say a piece at a Christmas program or an Easter program. Never. She couldn't walk—ever—so how would she get to the front of the church and up the steps to the platform? The old flame of hate flared up again, this time for Vi. She turned her back on both Vi and the baby.

Everyday after that Viola practiced her speech until Alice knew the words by heart and hated to hear the sounds. As the time drew near, Pa sent Vi way in to stand by the parlor double doors while he stayed in the kitchen.

"Now say it nice and loud," he said. "The church is big, you know, and they have to hear you way in the back." Viola giggled nervously and then shouted the words.

"Good, good," Pa said. "Do it that way."

At last the day came. Easter was to be celebrated on April 11, but the children's Easter program was scheduled for April 6, early in the evening.

"We'll all go," Pa decided. "The baby is big

136

enough to take along, and the weather is warm. It's just like city people to have a program at night, not thinkin' about us farmers. But I'll start the chores extra early so we can make it."

"How about Alice?" Ma asked. "Will you have to bring the go-cart?"

"No, I'll just carry her into church, and she can sit with us in the pew. She needs to get out o' the house more." He sent a warm smile toward Alice that almost melted her icy heart. "I can't say I agree with Dr. Banks about keepin' her quiet. She's just not a quiet child, though she's been quieter than usual lately."

So it was decided. Pa finished the chores early and hitched Nell to the buggy. Ma dressed Alice in her best dress and braided her stubby braids. Then she brushed Viola's glossy dark brown hair until it shone.

"Now I'll just dress the baby and put on my hat and we'll be ready," Ma said.

In spite of herself Alice was excited. She sucked in her breath with pain when Pa lifted her to the high seat, but she soon ignored her throbbing leg. She'd forgotten how much she could see from the buggy's high seat. Nell seemed to know that today was special too. Her harness straps gleamed, and the brass fittings sparkled in the sun. She stepped off proudly, and the buggy rattled down Sandy Hollow Road toward Rockford and Salem Swedish Church.

The church building was on the corner of Eighth Street and Fourteenth Avenue, just a block from busy Seventh Street where Ma and Pa did their shopping. The colored windows glowed in the late afternoon sun, and Alice's heart thumped in her chest when Pa pulled up smartly behind the church.

"Hurry Pa," Viola urged in her bossy grown-up way. "I have to meet my Sunday School class so we can all march in together."

"Yah, well you just wait till I help you down," Pa answered, "unless you want to get kicked or stepped on by a horse."

"Meet us back here right after the program," Ma said. "We'll want to get started home before it gets too dark." She turned in her seat and fussed with the big bow on the back of Viola's dress.

"Don't worry. I'll be here. Look for me when I march in." Taking Pa's hand Viola jumped down from the buggy and hurried off.

"—And be sure you speak up real loud." Pa's words were lost in the babble of voices as more

138

buggies turned into the yard. He spent a few minutes at the hitching rack, shaking his head at all the noise. Then he turned to take the baby so Ma could climb down from the buggy.

"Looks like the little fella's sleepin'," he said. "Hope he don't wake up in the middle of the program and start bellerin'."

Alice was the only one left in the high buggy now, and she looked down at the sleeping baby. He looked so sweet and cuddly. But he was already getting bigger, and the doctor's cruel words sounded in her ears . . . . "She'll never walk again . . . but he'll make a good farmer some day."

"I wish he'd never been born," she thought. And then she shivered, suddenly aware that Pa was speaking to her.

"Ready to go in, little one?" he said.

Alice nodded, though she hated the thought of being carried into church like a baby—big as she was. "Everyone will stare at me," she thought, "and then they'll whisper." But there was no other way, unless she stayed in the house on Sandy Hollow Farm all the time. She sighed and held out her arms.

Pa carried her easily. "You don't hardly weigh no more'n a thistledown," he teased. "But I got to watch for stickers." He followed Ma into the pew and settled Alice on the hard wooden seat. All the way down the aisle she had kept her face half hidden, but the peeks she'd taken over Pa's shoulder told her she'd been right. The grownups looked at her curiously or with pity. "There doesn't look to be anything wrong with her," the faces said, or "the poor child . . . she's the one who can't walk."

Now sitting down, Alice was like everyone else, and she craned her neck to look around. The cross on the wall gleamed in the light of the many electric lamps, lighted even though it was not yet dark outside, and the big audience of proud parents rustled in anticipation. Then the classes began to file into their front row seats.

The program began with a song by the primary class. Next, each of the little ones in the other classes shyly lisped out a few words of a piece. A few simply stood on the big platform and stared out at the audience. From where she sat in the middle of the church Alice couldn't hear most of the words, and she wiggled on the seat. Pa shook his head in warning and let his hand rest gently on her knee.

At last it was time for Viola's class of bigger girls. The class rose together and marched to the front. They sang a song, and their voices trembled on the notes. Then one by one each girl stepped forward exactly one step and spoke her piece.

Alice knew her sister's piece by heart, but she listened carefully to the others. At least these older girls spoke loud enough to hear. The words began to jumble together in her mind. "God loves us all . . . He understands . . . trust . . . we should love too . . . believe . . . forgive . . . love." The baby on Ma's lap stirred and whimpered, and Alice looked down at him. The old flame of hate flared up. But somehow that ugly feeling seemed out of place here, and she shifted her eyes uneasily away.

Viola stepped forward her one step. She was always so bossy and know-it-all, and Alice waited for her loud words, forming her own lips for what she knew she would hear. But Viola said nothing. She looked frightened, and her eyes darted around, searching for Ma and Pa. At last she looked right at Alice, and her eyes said, "Help me! I forgot!" Alice couldn't believe it. Why should she help?

Then, in spite of herself, she smiled and nodded her head, sitting up a little straighter. "*Jesu Kristu* . . . she mouthed the words. At once Viola picked them up and began her piece, smiling and speaking

141

even louder than she had from in front of the double
parlor doors.

>"Jesus Christ rose today
>And God had an angel say,
>'Come and see. He is not here.
>You no longer need to fear.' "

The program was over. The audience clapped as
the last class filed back to their seats, and everyone
but Ma and the baby—and Alice—stood to sing the
final hymn. The last organ note still hummed in the
air when Pa bent down and lifted Alice in his arms.

"Wasn't that fine?" His moustache brushed her
cheek. "And didn't Viola do a good job?"

Alice smiled back. Pa didn't realize that Vi had
forgotten her piece. But Alice knew that Miss Know-
it-all had been frightened. For once she'd needed help
from her little sister.

"Vi did the best job of all," she said. Pa
squeezed her a little and headed down the aisle ahead
of Ma and the baby.

Outside the air seemed heavy, and the sky was
dark though night had not yet come. Pa looked up,
squinting.

"I don't like the looks of that sky," he said.

142

"We might get rained on before we get home."

"Look Ma," Alice spoke as Pa set her down on the high buggy seat. "The sky is a funny color. It's sort of green."

"I see it." Ma shifted the baby from one arm to the other, and he began to cry. "Now where is Viola? She knows we have to hurry." She joggled the baby and patted him on the back. Pa was at Nellie's head stroking her nose and speaking soothing words in his deep voice. But Nellie stamped impatiently, and then she shuddered, tossing her head up and back. A rim of white showed around her rolled back eyes.

"Easy girl. Easy, Nellie." Pa spoke reassuring words, but he stayed at her head, gripping her bridle tightly with both hands. Around them in the church yard other horses whinnied and stamped in fear.

"Hurry Julia!" Pa called to Ma. "Go find Viola— quick as you can. We got to get out o' here, and I don't dare leave Nellie, or she'll bolt!"

Ma looked all around her, searching among the milling children for Viola. The rising wind lifted the brim of her hat and flapped it like a bird's wing. She reached up and set the blanket-wrapped baby on the buggy seat next to Alice.

"Just watch Larry for a minute, will you? I'll

be right back.'' She picked up her long skirt with one hand and hurried to the side entrance of the church. Alice looked down at her little brother. He'd stopped fussing now, and he stared back at her with big round eyes.

"... she'll never walk again ... but he'll make a good farmer some day ..." The words echoed in her mind.

Suddenly she looked up. A strange black horse broke away from his owner and dashed right in front of Nellie, rearing and pawing the air.

"Grab that horse!" a man yelled. Before the words were out, Pa dropped Nellie's bridle with one hand and lunged at the rearing horse. But the horse frightened Nell. She whinnied and lurched ahead in her traces, catching Pa off balance. The buggy jerked crazily, and the blanket wrapped baby slid toward the edge of the seat.

Alice gasped. For a second she hesitated, and the buggy jerked again. Then she grabbed the baby with both hands, bracing herself against the front seat with her good leg. The old hot pain raced up her bad leg, but she hung on grimly. Half off the seat, the baby wailed and arched his back.

"Don't worry," she whispered. "I won't let you

144

go. I love you!" Then she looked up. The buggy stopped jerking as Pa, with a set jaw and iron arms, forced both horses to a stand.

"*Tack sa mycket*, friend." A strange man hurried up and took over the trembling black horse. "I nearly lost him there. Something's got all these horses spooked bad."

"Yah, I think we ought to get out o' here and on the road." Pa still held Nell's head firmly. "Alice, are you all right?"

She unclenched her teeth. "Yes Pa, we're all right. Larry nearly fell off the seat, but I've got him."

"Hang on for just a minute more." He looked away. "Here comes your mother—finally."

Ma hurried through the crowd with Viola behind her, and Ma's brown eyes were snapping with anger.

"Get in the buggy," she said to Viola. "Here Alice. I'll take the baby. Why are you holding him so tight? It's making him cry."

"No, that's not why he's cryin'. He nearly got tossed out o' the buggy, and Alice caught him." Pa spoke from Nell's head. "Are we ready to go? Get settled in the seat, Julia, because Nell's goin' to run as soon as I let her go."

He let go the bridle and ran back to the buggy,

145

leaping into the seat just in time, for a jagged bolt of lightning ripped the Illinois sky open. Again Nellie started forward in terror, dragging the buggy after her. Its hard wheels clattered and skidded on the bumpy brick street, but the sound disappeared in the crack and boom of thunder. In the back seat Alice and Viola bounced about like bobbing apples. Alice shivered and opened her mouth, but no sound came out.

"Good thing you got in the buggy when you did, Pa!" Viola's dark eyes sparkled with excitement, and her brown braids flapped up and down. "Nellie almost ran away without you!" Ma turned part way around in her seat, clutching her church hat with one hand and holding on to the baby with the other.

"Hush, Viola. Pa has all he can do to manage the horse right now. If you hadn't dawdled, Nell wouldn't be so spooked. You girls button your coats up tight." She turned back to Pa. " Think it's goin' to rain before we get back to the farm?" He grunted and leaned back in the seat, pulling steadily on the reins.

"Whoa, Nell. Slow down, girl." As the horse's wild running slowed to a steady trot, he looked at Ma. Alice saw his mouth set in a grim line under the swoop of his moustache.

146

"Yah, it's goin' to rain and maybe more. We were fools to come to Rockford so late in the day."

"I suppose you're right, but you agreed—"

"I know," Pa said, "I agreed that the church Easter program was important." He sent a quick smile into the back seat. "I think you spoke your piece real good, Viola. I could hear you way back where I was sitting."

Viola smiled smugly at Pa's words, but Alice sighed and tucked her cold hands inside her sleeves like a muff. Always Viola—Viola or the baby. Then she thought of the baby sliding to the edge of the seat.

"He's so little," she said to herself. "He really needs me to look after him." She sat up a little straighter on the seat, ignoring the throbbing pain in her leg. "He needs a big sister like me." Another lightning flash lit up the evening sky, and the bare tree branches stood out in inky squiggles. She shivered again.

"Ma, Alice is shivering back here," Viola called out in her most grown-up voice.

"Am not!" Alice jabbed her sister with an elbow, but Ma turned around.

"It's no wonder. The temperature dropped way

down while we were in church for the program. Besides, you're sitting on the robe we brought along. Pull it out and wrap it around your legs."

Nell was trotting steadily now and had stopped tossing her head. Her long gray legs flashed in the gathering darkness as the buggy turned the corner of Harrison Avenue and Eleventh Street. Pa reached up and settled his hat more firmly on his head.

"Look at that sky to the east, Julia. There's a real storm comin'. That's why all the horses tied back o' the church were spooked. First I thought there'd been a dog back there stirrin' 'em up. But horses can sense a storm in the air. And it must be a bad one. I never saw Nell so wild. We'll be lucky if we get to the farm before we get wet. Wind's comin' up too."

Ma nodded. "It's a threatening sky all right. We better close the storm shutters on the house soon as we get home. Wind'll likely break a window otherwise."

The girls had been busily wrapping themselves in the itchy buggy robe while Ma and Pa talked. Now at last Alice began to feel warm, and the throbbing in her leg eased. She closed her eyes to keep out the lightning flashes, and soon her head began to nod.

GOD'S GREEN LINIMENT

The next thing she knew the wind had whipped off her bonnet and was shrieking in her ears. Pa's voice seemed to come from a long distance.

"It'll be a while before I get in. I gotta rub Nellie down with liniment and check the other animals."

"Oh Fred, do you have to?" Ma sounded worried.

"Yah, wild as Nell was, she'll be stiff otherwise. I'll hurry, but I want to make sure everything is fastened down. I don't like the looks of that sky!"

Fourteen

"Alice! Put your arms around my neck and hang on tight!" Ma's words were low but urgent, and Alice didn't hesitate. She wrapped her arms around her mother and felt herself lifted from the seat.

With Alice on one arm and the baby in the other Ma struggled up the porch steps against the wind. It pushed and tugged at their bodies. The maple trees along the driveway thrashed their bare branches and creaked and crackled. Suddenly, big drops of cold rain spattered on the wooden steps.

"Pull the door open, but hold on tight," Ma said to Viola. "That wind'll tear the door right out of your hands otherwise. There—in we go! Whew! Just made it. Now it's really starting to rain."

150

The glassed-in porch was dark and cold, but as soon as Vi opened the kitchen door, a wave of heavenly warmth rushed out from the big black cookstove. Ma lowered Alice to her go-cart seat and put the wailing baby in his cradle.

"You girls get your clothes off here in the kitchen and put your nightgowns on. It's already past your bedtime." She lifted the mantle of the kerosene lamp and lit the wide wick with a match. "This'll give you some light. Viola, see if you can stop Larry's crying. I got to help Pa get things fastened down outside. We're in for a bad storm."

Alice pushed her go-cart closer to the warmth of the cookstove. Her bonnet still hung by its ribbons down her back, and her ears ached from the wind.

"Weren't you listening, Alice? Get your coat off so you can get ready for bed." Ma's voice was sharp as she turned away to wrap a heavy shawl around her head and shoulders. Alice's eyes filled with tears, and hurried as she was, Ma noticed. "Now don't be scared," she said. "I'll be back in a few minutes." The door slammed behind her, and cold air swooshed into the kitchen.

Viola's eyes glittered in the shadows as she brought the nightgowns from the little bedroom off

151

the sitting room.

"Isn't this exciting?" she asked. "Oh, come on, Al, don't be a scaredy-cat."

BANG! A sudden noise outside made both girls jump.

"What was that?" Alice gulped.

"I don't know." Viola's voice quivered. Then she brightened. "Oh, look. That's only Ma closing the shutters. She said the wind might blow out a window otherwise." BANG! "See, there goes another one."

The baby wailed again, and Viola went to the cradle and rocked it with her foot. The wind shrieked around the corner, and a cold lump of fear weighed down Alice's middle as she tugged off her coat. Ma and Pa were out there somewhere in the screaming wind.

Viola hung her coat on a hook in the kitchen and began unbuttoning the row of buttons on her dress. "Bet you were scared when Nellie ran away so fast, weren't you?" she said.

"No, I wasn't scared," Alice insisted, though she knew she was fibbing. "I wasn't even scared—before you came—when Nellie bolted. Pa can make horses do what ever he wants." A picture of little Larry sliding off the seat flashed before her eyes, and she shivered.

152

"Let me hold the baby on my lap for a minute. He sounds like he's scared, he's crying so hard."

Viola set the baby on Alice's lap, and she held him tightly, patting him on the back with one hand. He looked up at her, and suddenly he stopped crying.

In the silence of the kitchen the noises outside seemed even louder than before. Both girls stopped to listen. "The wind is crying, too," Alice said. "And listen, the house is even shaking." Viola looked at her with big eyes, but she didn't say anything. Then the outside door banged shut, and Ma stood in the door-way.

"There," she puffed, "I fastened all the shutters tight, and Pa'll be in any minute." The kerosene lamp shone on her face, lighting up the wisps of hair torn loose from her bun. "Let's get you both in bed," she said. "Thank you for comforting the baby." She took Larry from Alice's lap and put him in the cradle. Then she pushed Alice through the darkened sitting room and into the bedroom. She pulled back the quilt and lifted Alice into bed. Then she bent down for a kiss and hurried out, her "Good-night!" trailing behind her. When she left, the shadows in the corners swelled and filled the room with darkness.

Alice pushed her nightgown down over her cold

153

feet and stuffed a finger in each ear. She whispered her nightly prayer: "Dear God, thank you for this day. Thank you for Pa and Ma and Viola and Larry." She stopped to think for a minute. "Please take good care of us . . . and . . . God, take care of Larry, 'cause he's too little to take care of himself. Amen."

She yawned a big yawn. Around her the farm-house creaked and shuddered, but Alice went to sleep. Soon she began to dream.

In her dream she was back in the buggy with the wind in her ears. She heard her father's words: "It'll be awhile before I get in. I gotta rub Nellie down with liniment . . . she'll be stiff otherwise."

Liniment. The big squarish bottle tipped, tipped again, and a big pool of green liniment spread out on Alice's hand. It was cold to the skin and stingy, and the smell of it—strong and puckery, a green smell—filled her nose. She wrinkled her nose in distaste and made a face, and then over the wind she heard Pa laugh.

"What's the matter?" he said. "I think this stuff smells good."

. . . She was in the horse barn now with Pa, and in this dream he was bending over Gypsy, the poor

154

lame horse. He poured some green liniment into the cup of his hand, and he began to rub Gypsy's leg. Up and down . . . up and down . . . Alice hitched herself to the edge of her seat.

"How come you rub her leg that way, Pa?" He looked up, squinting against the fumes of the liniment.

"One problem all horses have is poor circulation," he said. ". . . legs so long . . . hard for the blood to get all the way to the hoof. But when I rub 'em with this good green liniment, it makes the blood flow better, and then their hurt muscles or sore muscles can heal faster."

Liniment. The puckery smell made Alice's eyes water. She turned her head away, and in her dream she was back in her own bed again. Pa tilted the big green bottle, and the green liquid spread out like a stain. Up and down he rubbed on her aching leg . . . Up and down.

Liniment. The square bottle grew in size until it towered over her . . . tall as the windmill. In the back field the black iron beetle nodded its feeler and belched "clank-whoosh." Alice shivered . . . . The huge bottle tipped on its side, and a green liniment stain began to spread across the stubble field. The

155

beetle's feeler waved again . . . clank-whoosh . . . but the green stain spread nearer and nearer, and the air was filled with the sharp liniment smell. The iron beetle opened its jaw wide . . . clank! Then the green stain reached the beetle. The monster quivered once and was silent.

Liniment. Alice heard her mother's voice. "We've . . . we've been rubbing her leg with horse liniment."

". . . it doesn't seem to have hurt any." The doctor spoke, and the stinging smell disappeared. Then Dr. Banks spoke again.

". . . muscles are wasting away. But you should be glad you've got a healthy baby boy. He'll make a good farmer someday."

Alice whimpered, but in front of her the strange black horse reared, pawing the air. Then Nellie whinnied in fear, and the buggy lurched crazily. Before her eyes the baby slid toward the edge of the seat. Inside Alice the flame of hate was gone.

"Take care of him, God!" She shouted the words, grabbing the little bundle and hanging on . . . The buggy lurched again, and the wind howled.

The shutters rattled furiously, and the bed rocked on the shivering floor. Half awake and half asleep Alice opened her eyes. The wind was real, not a dream.

"Ma," she called, "the wind . . ." Through the door to the sitting room she saw the rosy glow of the lamp, and then her mother spread another quilt on the bed.

"It's all right, honey," Ma whispered, smoothing her forehead briefly. Alice clutched at her hand.

"The wind . . . will the wind blow us away?" She looked at Ma's pale face.

All at once the big house shuddered like a wounded animal. The walls quivered and shook in pain, and the shutters clattered like dry skeleton bones.

"Ma! What's happening?" Alice sat up with a start as Viola called from the sitting room. Ma's face twitched, and her hand on Alice's shoulder tightened and then let go.

"Viola, come in here and get in bed with Alice," she answered. "I got to get the baby."

Viola raced into the little bedroom and climbed into bed. Her hands were cold, and her face was pale. "Why, she's afraid too," Alice thought. In a minute Ma was back. She set the sleeping baby between the two girls and sat on the edge of the bed.

157

"It's all right; I'm here with you," she soothed. But her eyes were wide and black and her hands were shaking. "Fred!" she called, yelling Pa's name above the howling of the wind.

Again the walls swayed and cracked. This time the whole house seemed to move!

"Fred!" Ma called again. At last Pa ran into the room, swaying from side to side as he ran.

"I smothered the fire in the cookstove," he gasped, "so it can't start the kitchen on fire. I don't know if the house can hold up much longer!" He put his strong arms around Ma and the girls, holding them close in a circle—the baby in the hollow.

"Stay here, Fred," Ma's hands were icy. "Please stay here." Pa patted Ma's shoulder.

"Yah," he said. "I won't leave again. We ought to be in the cellar, but I don't dare take Alice down there in the damp and cold. We got to trust the Lord to protect us, 'cause there's no place else to go. I think we better all pray."

He bowed his head over Alice, and she could feel his lips moving on her hair. "Why the wind . . . it's just like my paralysis," she thought. "When it comes, there's nothing we can do." Then she bowed her head too, and her hand stole out to touch little

158

GOD'S GREEN LINIMENT

Larry.

"Please, God, I trust you . . . take care of the baby . . . please, God."

The whole family stayed that way for a long time—sitting on the bed in the little bedroom, praying and listening to the shrieking wind.

At last Pa lifted his head.

"Listen, Julia. I think the wind is letting up. Maybe the worst is over." Still the shutters banged and the house creaked, but the floor stopped shivering and the walls stayed still.

Finally, Ma sighed. "Thank the Lord, I think you're right. You girls get under the covers and go to sleep. Pa and I'll stay right here."

Later Alice woke with something digging in her side. She pushed Vi's elbow away irritably. "Get over on your own side of the bed," she muttered. Then she opened her eyes, realizing that it wasn't Vi's elbow after all, but her little brother's foot. "What's he doing here?" she thought, and she looked around.

One shutter hung half open, dangling from its hinges, and a greenish light streamed in through the window. More light came from a low-burning

159

kerosene lamp on the bureau. Alice lifted her head. "What—?" Pa was in the bedroom, fully dressed and sound asleep in his rocking chair! And in the other corner Ma curled awkwardly in the kitchen rocker. What were they doing in the bedroom?

She sat up with a jolt, rocking the bed and remembering the storm. "But it's over," she said to herself, "and Larry's all right. God did answer my prayer."

As soon as she moved, Pa opened his eyes and looked about him in a confused way. Then he leaped from his chair and ran in front of her to the window. The shutter dangled and swayed gently. The sun was just peeking over the trees, and the sunbeams bounced off a diagonal crack in the windowpane. Raindrops glinted on the brown grass.

"Look, Pa!" Alice cried. "Look! The hay wagon is in the garden! How'd it get over the fence?" Pa's tired eyes crinkled, and he turned from the window and hugged her close.

"We're lucky we're not scattered all over the garden too," he said. "We had a tornado last night; I'm sure of it. The wind must've picked up the hay wagon and lifted it right over the fence. I never seen anything like that before!"

160

By this time both Ma and Viola were awake and stretching. Ma looked at the baby on the bed and stumbled stiffly to the window. She peered out at the hay wagon and broken tree limbs with moist eyes.

"God was taking care of us last night," she said. "When the house shivered and shook so, I thought it would fly apart. I really expected it to be the end."

"We were lucky, weren't we, Ma?" Viola looked with big eyes at the hay wagon in the garden.

"No," Ma said, "it was more than luck. I think it was a miracle!"

While she was talking, Pa opened the window and leaned out over the sill. He turned back at once with a sharp exclamation.

"Yah, I'll say it's a miracle, Mother! Look out here. That wind pushed the house right off the foundation!" Ma bent out to look and drew a shaky breath.

"Good heavens, Fred, we'd better go see if there's anything left of the rest of the farm!" She hurried out behind Pa, but her voice floated after her. "We'll be back in a few minutes. Watch the baby so he doesn't fall off the bed!"

Alice bent over to look at her sleeping baby brother. His eyelids stirred and he sighed a tiny baby

161

sigh. "Miracle," she thought. "We asked for a miracle. And we got it."

Fifteen

Viola was out of bed and pulling her dress over her head.

"I'm going outside with Ma and Pa," she said. "Maybe the barn blew away!" Alice caught her breath, thinking of Nell and the other horses.

"Oh! I hope not. Listen—wait a minute. I can get in the go-cart, and I can go see too."

Vi looked at her doubtfully. "I bet you can't do it by yourself. And you're too heavy for me to lift."

"I can do it," Alice insisted. "Give me my dress and push the go-cart over here." Then she looked at Larry—just now waking up, and she grinned. "We'll have to take him too. He can ride on my lap."

163

With her dress on helter-skelter Alice pushed herself to the edge of the bed and swung her legs over the side. Then she stood up on one foot and turned, plopping into the chair of the go-cart. She looked at her sister triumphantly.

"See! Told you I could do it. Now give me the baby, and let's go!"

Viola pushed the go-cart through the sitting room and kitchen and out to the glassed-in entry porch, her unbuttoned shoes flapping against her legs. She threw open the door to the outside, and both girls stared.

The air felt light and washed clean, with none of yesterday's black-green threat. Twigs and branches littered the wagon yard and the driveway, and drops of water sparkled in the sun. The big barn and out-buildings that Grandpa had built way back in 1877 still stood solidly, but the metal windmill dangled like a broken tree branch from its high iron tower.

Suddenly Viola caught her breath. "Look Al, the corn crib's knocked down!" She raced down the steps and across the wagon yard. Alice looked down at Larry in her lap.

"At least the horse barn is all right. And so are you." She hugged him to her, and he squealed.

164

West of the hog house Pa and Ma stood looking at what once had been the corn crib. Splintered boards and shingles lay in heaps on the ground, and the one wall that stood tilted crazily.

"Pa," Alice called across the wagon yard, "Larry and I want to see too." Ma and Pa turned around with a surprised look. Then Pa hurried to the porch.

"Another surprise," he said. "You mean you got in the go-cart all by yourself? Hang on to the baby now. I'm goin' to tip you back and bump you down the stairs."

"Are the horses all right?" Alice asked as Pa pushed the go-cart over the gravel of the wagon yard.

"Snug as can be. Even Nellie is calmed down today. She sure was wild last night though. She knew what was comin', and she didn't want no part of it." Pa stopped the go-cart and stepped around in front of Alice. "I didn't get a chance to tell you last night, but I'm mighty proud of you, little one. You did just the right thing when that black horse went wild and spooked Nellie into runnin'. You kept your head and held on to the baby here. I didn't have time to tend to him, and I guess he'd 'a fallen out except for you." He put a big hand on her shoulder and squeezed gently. "You always have been my best helper."

Alice gulped and looked down at the baby in her lap. Did that mean Pa still needed her, even if she never walked? After all this time, it'd be a miracle if she ever could stand on that leg again. A miracle. An idea tickled the back of her mind, but she couldn't see it clearly. Pa went back behind the go-cart and pushed it to the ruins of the corn crib. Ma reached down and took the baby.

"The corn crib's a complete loss, isn't it?" she asked.

Pa frowned. "Yah, I'll have to tear it down and build a new one. And I'll have to do it this summer. But—" his face brightened, "it's not so bad. Wasn't much fodder left in it, bein' so late in the year, and the machinery was all out. Besides, the big barn wasn't hurt, so the animals are all right." He put a hand on Ma's shoulder. "We had worse damage to the house. Wait till Grandpa sees that."

Ma gasped and turned to clutch Pa's hand. "Oh Fred, do you think he's all right? What if the tornado went through Rockford too? I'm so glad we got a telephone. I'm going to ring him up right now!" She picked up her skirts with one hand and ran to the house, the baby joggling over her shoulder. Pa shook his head.

"Bet the wind blew the telephone lines down," he called. Then he turned back. "Viola, you stay away from the rubble now. There's nails sticking up from the boards, and I don't want you hurt. We'll go over to the house, and I'll show you what happened there." He looked up as Ma appeared in the doorway. Her face was white and pinched.

"I can't get the operator, Fred. The line is dead."

Pa nodded grimly. "Lines are down. I'll have to drive in there to see if he's all right. But we got to milk first, and we better all have some breakfast." He pushed the go-cart back to the house and pointed to the foundation stones.

"See here," he said. "The house is supposed to sit snug on top o' the foundation. But the wind blew so hard last night it lifted the whole house right up in the air—moved it about six inches, and then set it back down again." He bent over. "Look, you can see right into the cellar through the gap. On the other side the walls are leaning over the edge." He straightened up and smiled. "But it's nothin' that can't be fixed, and we're all right and so are the animals. Praise the Lord for that!"

Pa hurried through breakfast and milking,

pushed by Ma's white face and her worry about her father in town. Years ago Grandpa had lived in this very house and Ma had been his little girl. Now he was too old to be a farmer, and he had moved to Catlin Street in Rockford to be near his old friends. Alice itched to go see him. Maybe exciting things had happened in Rockford. Maybe the tornado had blown houses down!

"Please, Pa, let us go to town with you," she begged.

"Please, please," Viola echoed.

"I should say not. If there's trouble in town the last thing I want is two little girls underfoot. Besides, I need Viola to help clean up the yard. You pick up all the broken branches and pile 'em by the garden fence in a big pile. Alice, you help Ma in the house." He pushed his plate away and stood up. "When I get home, I'll take the garden fence down and pull the hay wagon out. Now don't worry," he said to Ma, "I'll be back as quick as I can."

In spite of his promise to be quick, the hours dragged by, and Pa didn't come home. Noon time came and went, strangely quiet without his big appetite and his jokes. After dinner Alice wiped the dishes while Viola picked up twigs and dragged

168

broken branches to the fence. Only a few branches had blown down from the big maple, but in the front yard a whole box elder tree lay on its side like a great wounded bird. Thick roots slithered claw-like through the tangled ball of earth, and a big muddy hole scarred the lawn.

Alice was hanging the dish towel on its hook when Viola burst into the house.

"Pa's coming!" she cried. "I can hear the buggy." A few minutes later Nellie trotted briskly up the graveled driveway. Ma hurried to the door, and Pa swept off his hat and waved.

"Grandpa's all right," he shouted. "Whoa, Nell."

Ma sighed with relief and dropped her hands to her side.

"Wasn't any damage on Catlin Street at all," he continued, "but the telephone lines are all down. Electricity is out too." He grinned. "See, we're better off without modern conveniences like electricity. When you really need 'em, they don't work." He reached in his coat pocket. "Here, I brought both newspapers so you could read about the storm. I'll unhitch and be in shortly." He slapped the reins on Nell's back. "Gid-dap."

Ma came into the kitchen, unfolding the

newspapers. She spread them out on the table and scanned the front pages quickly. Then she set the *Rockford Register-Gazette* aside and bent her head to read the *Daily Republic*. Alice looked at the straight rows of letters marching across the pages. She still couldn't read because she couldn't go to school, and it made her squirm not knowing what secrets those rows of letters held. She turned to her sister.

"Read to me, Vi. What does it say?" Viola pointed to a row of numbers just under the big black headlines.

"That's the date. See, it says April 7, 1909."

"Is that today?" Alice asked.

"Yup. Now listen." She began to read. "**AN EX—PEN—SIVE APRIL WIND.** Oh," she complained, "these words are too hard for me to read." Ma looked up.

"What is it? I'll read it to you," she said. Pointing with her finger to the words under the big black headline, she read:

"MINIATURE DAYLIGHT HURRICANE STRIKES CITY AND CAUSES THOUSAND DOLLARS DAMAGE— *WEST END FURNITURE FACTORY ROOF BLOWN OFF. PHONES AND ELECTRIC LIGHTS OUT OF ORDER."*

170

"A thousand dollars damage!" Alice couldn't imagine so much money.

"Shh. Listen to this."

"The Electric Company hadn't an arc wire intact in the north or west end of Rockford at noon. Manager Golding announced, however, that by night every light would be burning.

The wind struck the city last night about 10:30 o'clock, raged savagely and cut up antics and passed stationary things at the velocity of about 40 miles an hour. Things which were not loose—and these included people—were jerked along at a speed which would violate the automobile ordinance at any other time."

"What's that mean, Ma?"

Ma laughed. "That means the wind was blowing faster than folks are allowed to drive their autos on city streets." She folded the newspaper. "But it must have been blowing harder than that here. I think we had more damage on this one farm than they did in town. The wind must have hit here first and then gone into Rockford. Guess it wasn't a tornado though. The paper calls it a hurricane. Maybe nobody saw a funnel cloud." She looked up as Pa shut the door behind him. "I'm glad Grandpa wasn't hurt."

171

"No he's all right. Said he had to scratch around and dig out his old kerosene lamp, though, when the electricity failed. Good thing he kept it. I always said we're just as well off without electricity here on the farm. That way we don't count on it."

Ma interrupted. "They say it wasn't a tornado."

"Yah," Pa answered, "but I see by the paper they did have tornadoes in Indiana yesterday. We just got the winds and rain. Pretty strong winds though." He pulled out a chair and sat down.

"I stayed in town long enough to ask Grandpa for advice about gettin' the house moved back. He says he knows how to do it, and if I bring the wagon into town tomorrow I can pick up the jacks and timbers he's got stored in his little barn. Then he'll come out and help me move the house."

"Can the two of you do it without help, Fred?" Ma looked worried, but Pa laughed.

"Course we can. Your father didn't work in the iron mines all those years without learnin' about jackin' up heavy things and movin' 'em around." He stroked the pointed ends of his beautiful moustache. "Well, I can't sit here gassin'. That storm made work for me, that's what it did. The way the wind was blowin', it's a miracle the whole farm didn't get

172

blown flat."

Miracle. That word again. Suddenly Alice remembered the dream she'd had while the wind howled around the house. In her mind she could smell the stingy green liniment, and she saw the green stain spreading across the stubble field.

"Did you rub Nellie with green liniment last night, Pa?" she asked. He stopped halfway out of his seat and looked at her.

"Yah," he said, "I did. Hated to take the time to do it in the middle of the storm, but I knew she'd be stiff and aching otherwise."

"And this morning . . . was she limping when she took you to town?"

Pa laughed. "Not a bit. She skimmed along the road like she was flyin'. Why do you want to know?"

Alice searched for the right words. "Remember Pa, when my leg first started hurting—right after threshing. Didn't—didn't you rub my leg with horse liniment then?" Pa looked at Ma and nodded his head slowly.

"Yah, we did it to bring down your fever. And it did seem to work."

"Well—if that green liniment works for Nellie when she's sore, wouldn't it work for my sore leg

173

too?"

Pa stared at Alice, slowly rolling his moustache point between his fingers. Ma took Alice's hand in her own.

"Honey, the doctor said there was no use in rubbing your leg once the fever was gone. He said the best thing to do was to keep it still to rest the muscles." Pa looked at Alice strangely for a long minute.

". . . and we did what the doctor said, and now the muscles are wastin' away!" He clapped his hand to his forehead and groaned. "I've been a fool, Julia. Why should her leg be any different from a horse's leg? Of course she's right. What that leg needs is massage, rubbin',—stimulation to get the blood movin' . . . " Then he looked right into Alice's eyes.

"Maybe we've had more'n one miracle today. I ain't sayin' that rubbin' your leg is goin' to work, but we're goin' to try it. I never stopped believin' that someday you'd walk again, but it's been lookin' pretty bad." He stood up and thumped his hand on the table.

"Get the green liniment, Julia. Tomorrow we'll get your house settled back on its foundation. But right now I'm goin' to start rubbin' this filly's leg!"

174

Sixteen

The next morning Alice heard the cookstove grate rattle while it was still black as shoe polish outside. Pa finished the chores in record time and stopped in the house only long enough to rub her leg with green liniment.

"Got to hurry today," he said, rolling his sleeve part way up his arm. "Now you just lay back there and relax." He unscrewed the top from the liniment bottle and poured some liniment in his hand. Then he rubbed both hands together, just as though he washed them. A bit of liniment dropped on Alice's good leg, and she shivered.

"Oooh Pa. That's cold!"

"Yah, liniment is funny stuff. When you put it on, it's cold. But after you rub it in, it makes you warm."

Now Pa began to rub the bad leg, and Alice watched him. His hands were so big they wrapped all the way around her leg, so with each up and down stroke her leg went into the tunnel of his hands. Her eyes began to water from the strong green smell, but just as she was about to complain, Pa stopped rubbing and wiped his hands on a towel.

"That's it for now," he said. "I'll rub it again this afternoon. You get dressed now." He bent down and kissed her on the cheek.

A few minutes later he set off for town in the wagon with Blackie and Prince pulling.

"Good thing it's Easter vacation," Viola said, "or I'd have to go to school today, and I'd miss all the excitement. I don't see how Pa is going to move a whole house."

"Maybe he'll use the horses. They're big and strong." Alice turned to her mother. "Ma, can I go outside today so I can watch? Please?" Ma smiled and nodded.

"I think we can manage that. Vi can push you around."

At midmorning Pa and Grandpa were back at Sandy Hollow Farm, the wagon piled high with long round poles, heavy timbers, and rusty iron machines. Alice and Viola were already outside, and when Grandpa stepped down from the wagon, he greeted them in Swedish.

"*God morgan*, young'uns," he said. "Understand you're good sleepers. Slept through most of the hurricane, I hear." He pulled off his hat, and his bald head shone in the sunlight. "Smart girls. Can't do anything about a hurricane. Might as well sleep." He turned to Pa. "Let's take a look at that foundation, 'fore we decide where to drop those poles. At my age I don't want to carry 'em if I don't have to."

"What're those big poles for?" Alice asked. "Can you push the house with them?"

"No, they're rollers," Pa answered. "We're goin' to jack the house up with timbers. Then we'll stick these rollers underneath and roll it back on the foundation where it belongs." He waved his hand. "Viola, you push the go-cart over there. Otherwise you'll both be in the way. Scat now!"

The work went on and on, though nothing seemed to be happening. Pa pushed up and down on a pole stuck in a rusty machine—like pumping water— and Grandpa shoved in a timber. Then they moved to another corner of the house and did the same thing.

177

"I can't see where they're doing anything. They'll never get the house moved this way." Viola flopped on the long bench under the maple tree.

"When do you think they'll get the horses?" Alice asked, for she was sure that only Blackie and Prince were strong enough to move the house. Just then she heard Grandpa's voice.

"Yah, that oughta do it, Fred. Now let me go to the other side and make sure it's lined up. We only have to move the rollers once if we do it right." He disappeared around the corner of the house. "Now just a little push," he called.

Push . . . move poles . . . inspect . . . discuss. Still the work went on. Alice stared out across the orchard. The branches of the apple trees were red against the greening grass—swelling and ready to burst into bloom. She looked up as Pa came toward her.

"Did you see the house move, little one?" he asked.

"Move? It didn't move."

Pa laughed. "Yah, it moved all right. It's right back where it's supposed to be. Now we only have to let it down." He pushed his cap back on his forehead. "Mean to tell me we moved the house, and you didn't even know it?"

"She was waiting for the horses to come, Pa," Viola said.

"Didn't need any horses," Pa answered. "Just some simple tools, Grandpa's know-how, and patience to do the job right—a little at a time. Y'know, God works that way too. Did you ever see a corn stalk grow? You can't see it growin', but if you measure, sometimes it'll grow six inches in one day. That's God workin'." He rubbed his fingers along the swoop of his moustache. "Viola, you run to the milkhouse and tell Ma that her house movin' is just about finished!"

The whole spring went like the house moving. When Pa took on a job, he did it thoroughly, and Alice began to be sorry she had mentioned the liniment. Four or five times a day either Ma or Pa dropped what they were doing and came with the big squarish bottle to rub her leg. The whole house and all her clothes reeked with the strong green smell.

"What makes that liniment smell so strong, Ma?" Alice asked at one of the rubbing sessions. Ma looked over her spectacles and smiled.

"Your Pa would say the strong smell is on

purpose to wake up the blood in your leg and make it move around. But it's what's in the liniment that makes it smell. Let's see—" she took a deep breath. "I think I smell peppermint camphor and—I know. It's wormwood."

Alice shivered. "Ugh. What's wormwood anyway?"

Ma shook her head. "I don't know exactly, but I know it comes from a herb and it's dark green and bitter tasting. But you don't have to drink it, so it doesn't matter. You only have to smell it."

Even worse than the smell, though, was the ache in her leg. Before, it had stopped hurting except for an occasional twinge, but now it began to ache again as it had not ached since last winter. "It's getting worse!" Alice thought. Several times she nearly asked Pa to stop rubbing because it hurt so, but then she remembered. Nothing else she'd tried had worked, and she was determined to get to school in the fall. Pretty soon she'd be too old! But the rubbing went on, day after day, and nothing happened.

Around the farm, though, little by little, things were changing. The windmill again whirred busily on its high stand. Pa worked and worked, and suddenly one day the corn crib's leaning wall disappeared, and

a new corn crib began to rise up. The box elder tree in the front yard turned into a neat stack of firewood for the cookstove. Pa filled in the muddy hole it had left, and he planted grass seed in the dirt.

And then there was Gypsy. All spring Pa had

spent many extra hours working with the roan horse.
He had given her an extra ration of oats every day
until her bony flanks began to round out. He had
brushed and curried her coat until it took on a glossy
sheen, setting off the reddish color.

In May he had called in the blacksmith. Pa often
did his own shoeing, but this time the smith trimmed
the hoofs of every horse on Sandy Hollow Farm and
made new shoes for them. Last of all, he trimmed
Gypsy's hoofs and made a specially shaped shoe for
the sore leg.

"That'll ease the strain on those leg muscles,"
the smith said. "She'll be walking without a limp
before long."

All winter and spring Pa had been faithfully rubbing Gypsy's leg with the awful-smelling horse
liniment, the same liniment he was using now on
Alice's leg. A month after the new shoe was put on,
he announced that Gypsy was cured.

"I'll pass the word when I'm in town that I got
a top-notch buggy horse for sale," he said. "Then
we'll see if I made a good investment."

Two days after Pa's announcement a horse
buyer came from Rockford. He turned off Sandy
Hollow Road, tied his horse to the hitching post, and

knocked on the door. Alice was in the orchard in her go-cart, and she itched to hear what her father was saying. But he was too far away, so she could only watch as Pa led Gypsy around the wagon yard to show off her good form. Then he hitched her to the buggy, and the two men sped down the drive and onto the road for a demonstration ride.

Later, when Pa came in the house for dinner, he was whistling. He grabbed Ma by the waist and whirled her in a circle.

"Mother," he said and his eyes were shining, "I just sold Gypsy and earned us two hundred dollars! Now what d'you think of your horse-trading husband?"

Ma spoke sharply. "I think you're a scalawag, Fred Lindstrom!" Then she laughed. "But you're a smart one, I have to admit that!"

"The liniment worked on Gypsy," Alice thought to herself, "but it doesn't seem to do anything for me." She sighed. "Pa can do anything—fix a horse, fix a house, build a corn crib. If only he could fix me!"

Once in a while, though, Alice was able to forget that she "wasn't fixed." Just as they'd done before she got sick, the family gathered each week around

183

the sitting room table to clean and buff the horses' brass harness fittings. Pa insisted that the brass trappings on each piece of harness must be polished until they gleamed. And he inspected each one!

"Fred, you're a regular old fuddy-duddy about your harness," Ma often said, but Alice could hear the smile in her voice as she said it.

Pushed up to the table in her go-cart, Alice was like everybody else. The powerful gasoline lamp made a bright circle of light, and everybody's fingers rubbed busily. It was hard and grubby work and Pa was exasperating sometimes. But usually his eyes twinkled as he rubbed, and he made everybody laugh by telling stories about his boyhood in Sweden.

One night Pa looked around the table and cleared his throat. "Here's a question for you girls," he said. "Can you tell me how many Swedes are sons?" His soft brown hair gleamed amber under the light, and his moustache ends poked out saucily.

"I know," Viola said, showing that she went to school and was smart. "All of them are sons that aren't daughters."

"Aha," Pa replied, "what about Hannah Carl*son*? Isn't she a *son*? And then there's Edda Ander*son* and Hulda John*son*."

"Pa, you're cheating," Alice giggled. Those're just their names. That doesn't have anything to do with making them sons."

"But it does," Pa answered. "Let me tell you a little story."

"My Pa's first name was Per. When I was born, I was named Frederick, and since I belonged to Per, I was called Per's son. Way back in 1872 when I was born, nobody in Sweden had last names. There were Axels and Johns and Peters and Svens, and since there weren't many people in our little village, everybody knew who everybody else was anyhow."

"What happened if more than one boy had the same name?" Vi asked.

"That's when the problem started," Pa said. "As soon as we had two Erics . . . bang! . . . there was trouble. But those smart Swedes solved that problem. The Eric who lived down the road from us was the son of Carl, so he was known as Eric Carlson. The Eric who lived by the creek was the son of John, so people started calling him Eric Johnson. All of a sudden we had last names!"

Alice sat quietly for a minute, her hands still and her forehead puckered in concentration. "That's why Grandpa's name is Peterson!" she shouted, suddenly understanding. "His pa's name must've been Peter."

"You're right, Alice," broke in Ma, stopping her flashing knitting needles for a minute. "And my pa's father—your great-grandfather—was Peter Erickson."

Alice's head whirled with all the names she knew that suddenly had new meanings. But Vi seemed puzzled.

"Pa, what about Gustaf Froberg? He's a Swede. Where'd his last name come from?"

Pa pursed his lips. "Ummm . . . I don't know the answer to that for sure. Let's see, *fro* means from and *berg* means mountain. Maybe his folks in Sweden lived on a mountain." He tossed a bridle on the pile in the center of the table and picked up a leather strap. "I can tell you a story about a name I do know the answer to though. What's your last name?"

"It's Lindstrom," Viola answered quickly. "Pa that's not a *son* name either, and we're Swedes!"

"That's where the story comes in."

"Oh Pa, tell us. Tell us." Both girls chimed in together.

"Once upon a time, many many years ago," Pa began in his deep story-telling voice, "I was a little boy in Staldalen, Sweden. Then I was known as Frederick, Per's son. But guess what? My father was known as Per, Frederick's son, because my grandpa's name was like mine—Frederick. That got a little mixed-up, but we managed. Like I said, all the people in the village knew everybody else anyhow."

"When I was about twenty years old, I had to quit my job at the iron mines and go off to be a soldier in the army." He looked up, his eyes twinkling. "You know, Sweden's been a peaceful country for hundreds of years. It hasn't fought any wars, but it's always had a big strong army. In my day every Swedish boy had to serve in the army three months each year for three years, and he had to start when he was twenty."

"Weren't you scared, Pa?" Vi looked at him with big round eyes.

He laughed. "No, I wasn't scared. It was somethin' everybody had to do. They put me in the cavalry, and I really liked that 'cause my job was takin' care of the horses. We'd been too poor to have a horse on our farm when I was growin' up, so this was my first chance to learn about horses. And talk about spirit—some o' those horses were as proud as the king."

"But," Pa interrupted himself, "I was tellin' you about names. When I went in the army they called me

187

Frederick Person, with the words all run together. Just like that I had a last name! Trouble was, lots of other soldiers had fathers named Per, so there were lots of Persons. I wouldn't have minded so much, but —wouldn't you know it—in my outfit another soldier had the very same name I did!"

"Pa, your name's not Frederick Person." Alice was worried now. "It's Frederick Lindstrom."

"Hold on. I'm gettin' to that," he answered. "Anyhow, back then in the army my name was Frederick Person, and in the same outfit was another young soldier named Frederick Person. Somebody'd yell 'Fred' and I never knew whether they were callin' me or not." He stopped polishing for a minute, and his teasing voice grew serious.

"As if that wasn't bad enough, one day that other Fred came up to me holdin' a letter that'd been opened. He looked at me with a silly grin on his face, and then he said kinda high and squeaky, 'Dear Fred, I miss you so much. I can scarcely wait till you get home again.' "

"I tore that letter out o' his hand and studied it. Sure enough, my girl friend back in Staldalen had written it. She'd addressed it to Frederick Person, only he'd gotten it instead o' me." He thumped on

188

the table. "I felt like knockin' him down, I was so mad. Still, it wasn't his fault, except for teasin' me. There were just too blamed many Persons in the Swedish army."

"What did you do?" Alice asked.

"Right quick I changed my name! I got rid of the name Person and made it Lindstrom. Lindstrom sounded like a good name, and there weren't very many of 'em around. My ma got mad at me, but she couldn't do anything."

"How did you ever pick that name?" Viola asked. Pa looked at her and chuckled.

"Guess I made it up," he said. "In Swedish *lind* comes from linden-tree. That's a tree with yellow flowers and leaves shaped like hearts. So then I thought of trees, and lots o' times they grow by water, right? So I added *strom*, 'cause *strom* means stream." He laughed out loud. "So our name means linden-tree-stream. Doesn't make much sense, does it? But it's better'n bein' just one of a hundred Persons." He shook out a waxy rag and rubbed the strap furiously. Then he went on.

"Some soldiers went back to their old names when they got out o' the army, but I kept the new one. So when I left Sweden and came to America, I came as Frederick Lindstrom. A few years later I took out my papers to be a citizen of the United States. That made the Lindstrom name legally mine."

"I'm glad we have our very own last name," Viola said.

"Me too," Alice echoed, dreamily pushing a bit of rag over a brass buckle. In her mind she saw a whole parade of Swedes marching down Seventh Street in Rockford. They came in ranks: Anderson, Ericson, Abramson, Peterson, Swanson, Hanson, Axelson, Johnson, Swenson, Paulson, Jacobson, Nelson, and —yes, Person. But leading the parade, ahead of all the rest, marched her family—the Lindstroms. Pa marched proudly, holding Viola and Alice each by a hand, and Ma carried little Larry. What a grand dream!

Then with a gulp she suddenly remembered her crippled leg. Would she ever be able to walk, let alone march? She bent her head.

"Oh God," she prayed under her breath, "please heal me with that liniment like you healed Gypsy. Pa's been rubbing my leg for ever so long, and it's not getting any better. Now it's almost summer, and I can't feel anything, and I can't step on it. I'll be patient if you want, but someday please heal me!"

Seventeen

The pale green days of spring gave way to crayon green days in June, and the pain in Alice's leg grew worse. The green liniment smell hung in the humid air like a cloud, following her wherever she went. She hated the smell and she hated the rubbing, and though she tried every morning when she rolled off the edge of her bed, her leg wouldn't support her weight. It crumbled under her like a dry biscuit.

School was out for the summer—a whole year wasted!—and Viola was home every day.

"Vi'll push you around the wagon yard now that school's out," Pa said as he pushed her go-cart down the porch steps and outside. "You can play out here all day, and it'll be almost as good as bein' able to walk."

Alice nodded. He tried so hard to cheer her up, but he didn't understand. "It's not the same at all," she thought, "and I hate to ask Vi to push me.

191

Besides what can I do sitting in a dumb old chair? I can't hunt for kittens in the barn. I can't play tag, and I can't climb trees." She looked up bitterly as her big sister burst out the door and ran down the steps. "And I can't run down the steps either." She clenched her teeth. Patience, Pa had said.

"Let's go see the baby pigs," she called. "Pa said he let them out of the pen this morning." Vi was nearly across the driveway, but she turned back, kicking at a clump of grass with her bare toes.

"After while I will. Now I want to go swing."

"Pa said you have to push me!" Alice shrieked the words—loud enough so Ma was sure to hear, and she beat a tattoo with her fists on the arms of her go-cart.

"No, I don't. Not all the time. Besides, today's my first day of vacation." Vi tossed her head and turned away. "I'm not going to be tied down all summer with you!"

"Viola!" Ma stood in the porch doorway with her brown eyes shooting sparks. "I heard what you said, and you better change your tune. Tied down! You don't know how lucky you are." She shook a threatening finger. "Alice was stuck in the house all winter while you went to school. Now she needs to get out in the fresh air and sunshine. And you push her around the yard, miss, or you'll have me to deal with!" She went back into the house, slamming the door behind her. Vi stuck out her tongue at her mother's back and then turned to Alice.

"Now see what you did," she hissed. "I was only teasing anyhow. Okay, let's go see the dumb old pigs!" She went behind the go-cart and started it forward with a jerk.

Like a summer thunderstorm, the quarrel seemed to clear the air. Or maybe Ma had a talk with Viola that Alice didn't hear. Whatever it was, after that first fight, summer turned into fun. The monotonous rubbing went on as before, and the liniment smell that hung around Alice blocked out all the good summer smells. But Vi invented games that Alice could play in her go-cart, and she taught her to braid clover chain necklaces, adding a new pinkish-white blossom whenever the short stem of one was braided in. Even better, she taught Alice how to balance on one foot, so she could hop short distances with all her weight on her good leg. How exciting it was to be out of the go-cart! When Alice got good at hopping, the girls had hopping contests, and sometimes Alice actually won. Sometimes too they had tea parties, and they played store with pebbles for money and black-eyed Susans for store goods.

Best of all, one summer afternoon—July it was— they had a hollyhock wedding.

Ma was too busy to plant a regular flower garden. Between house and barn chores and the vegetable garden, she scarcely ever had a spare minute. But somewhere she scrimped enough time to plant a few bits of color here and there around the house. On either side of the front door she dug a small flower bed. In the center Ma planted asters— glorious fringed flowers of purple and pink and white and burgundy. Around the edges white and pink petunias marched in a riot of fuzzy stems and fragile belled blossoms. And along the fence at the east side of the house morning glories and hollyhocks grew on their own every year.

"You don't plant morning glories or hollyhocks," Ma said. "They grow where they please, but somehow they seem to plant themselves."

Morning glories were blue—the clear deep blue of a summer sky. They opened like trumpets, flinging the edges of their petals outward to show the delicate inner tracing of white that led to the center. They

194

grew on a vine up the fence, twining in mad profu-
sion, tumbling over one another, and mixing up their
leaves. Every morning the blossoms opened their blue
faces to the blue sky and the warm sun. But in the
evening, when the sun hid its face in the west, the
flowers hid too, pulling together their trumpet petals
and folding up like an umbrella.

"Morning glories are pretty to look at," Alice
thought, "but hollyhocks are better, 'cause you can
do things with them." Hollyhocks grew stiff and tall,
so tall they sometimes towered above even Pa's head.
The stem was as thick and tough as a tree branch at
the bottom but thinned and grew tender near the top,
until it ended with a rounded flower bud at the very
tip. The stem had spines with little fuzzy fringes, and
the leaves grew big and round as plates, dark green
near the ground and shading to lighter green near the
top. At each joint of the straight stalk a small stem
jutted out to hold a flower.

Best of all were the colors. Hollyhocks came in a
red so dark it was almost purple, in rose red, in deep
pink, in middle pink, and in a pink as pale as a baby's
eyelid. They came in pure white, in white edged with
red or pink, and in pale lemon yellow. Alice had
never seen a blue hollyhock, but she thought, "Some-

where God must have made one."

That morning Viola pushed the go-cart to a shady spot under the elm tree. "What shall we do today?" she asked. Then she caught her breath. The hollyhocks along the fence were at their peak, with hundreds of multi-colored blossoms sprouting from the stiff stems. "Let's have a wedding," she said—and in the next breath, "I get to make the bride!"

Alice's smile wilted, but Viola noticed and said generously, "You decide what colors to use. I'll go find a burdock leaf for a carpet."

She ran across the yard to search in the field. "Here, isn't this a beauty?" she called a few minutes later, waving a huge dark green leaf.

"That's rhubarb! Ma'll be mad if you pick her rhubarb," Alice called back. But Vi shook her head as she came closer.

"No, it's not rhubarb, dummy. See—" She turned the big leaf over. "Rhubarb leaves are smooth on the bottom, and burdock is all fuzzy like this. And besides," she smiled knowingly, "rhubarb stems are pink, not dark green like this one." With one quick motion she split the leaf open with her fingernail, flattening it enough to spread out on the grass.

Alice still wasn't convinced. "What's burdock

good for anyhow?" she asked. Her sister laughed.

"Nothing, I bet. You sure can't eat it. But it'll make a dandy carpet for our wedding." She looked up at the hollyhocks. "Did you pick a color?"

"Yes, but there's so many. Let's each do a wedding." Alice turned anxiously to Vi. "I want to do mine pink!"

"All right, I don't care. I'll get another burdock leaf for you. Do you still remember how to do it? You were pretty little when I showed you last year." She grinned as Alice sputtered angrily, and she pushed the go-cart right up to the fence.

When she left, Alice studied the hollyhocks carefully. She decided to have a big wedding with a maid of honor and three bridesmaids—maybe even a tiny flower girl, and of course the bride. From the middle of a tall hollyhock stalk she pinched off a blossom of purest white, leaving a bit of stem sticking out for the bride's neck. She turned the blossom upside down on her lap and reached higher up the same stalk for a bud nearly ready to pop open. She left no stem on the bud, but peeled away the green bud cover, exposing tiny almond-shaped black eyes at the base of the folded white petals. Then she carefully pushed the bud on to the pointy stem end of the big

197

flower.

"Finished!" she said. The bride's snowy gown swooped out grandly from her shoulders, and the crown of her matching white headdress rose high above her lustrous black eyes. "See!" She held out the bride at arm's length. "Told you I remembered how! Put her on the carpet for me, please."

Viola arranged the bride in the center of the burdock leaf, spreading her skirts daintily around her.

"That's pretty good," she said. "I think I'll dress my bridesmaids in shades of yellow." She walked down the fence row and squatted near a cluster of yellow hollyhocks.

Alice hummed happily to herself, picking three hollyhock blossoms of the very same size and the very same shade of pink. "You'll make beau-tiful bridesmaids," she whispered. "You must be very rich." With the same care she'd lavished on the bride, she peeled small pink buds for each headdress and fitted them on to the stem necks. Then she bent over as far as she could reach without toppling and dropped them very gently on the burdock leaf, two on one side of the bride and one on the other.

Just then Vi came back and knelt next to her

leaf, arranging four flower bridesmaids along its edge. They wore elegant pale yellow gowns with towering yellow-orange headdresses. Alice bent to watch.

"What're the dandelions for?" she asked.

"Bouquets." Viola carefully poked a hole half-way down the petal skirt and inserted a tiny golden dandelion. "See, that makes them even better." She rocked back on her heels and looked at Alice's wedding party. "Yours are pretty though. Now if we only had a groom."

"How about tying sticks together with grass?"

"It won't work. I tried it before, and they just fall apart. I know," Vi finally said. "I'll ask Ma if we can use wooden clothespins."

She returned a moment later clutching two clothespins. "Look! She even gave me a pencil to put on faces with. But she said to be sure not to break them, 'cause we can't have any more." She held out a clothespin, complete with eyes and mouth.

"Where's mine?" Alice asked.

Viola held out her other hand. "Here, you put on your own face. I still got to find a tiny flower for my flower girl." She leaned her groom against the bride and wandered off down the fence row.

Alice held her clothespin tight and concentrated

on drawing a face on the rounded top. "You need a long curvy moustache, just like Pa," she whispered. "There! Oh, you're handsome!" She leaned over to set him down, and when she did, she noticed that Viola's groom had fallen over onto his face. Quickly she picked him up and set him upright. Again he toppled over.

"Maybe if I spread his legs out a little more . . ." she thought, and she pulled at the wooden pieces.

SNAP! Suddenly one leg of Viola's groom broke right off.

"Oh!" Alice said to herself. "Now I did it! And Ma said we can't have any more clothespins. Good thing it wasn't mine that broke. *My* groom still has both legs. But Vi'll be mad."

She sat still then, looking at the broken clothespin in one hand and the perfect groom with his moustache in the other, and she was ashamed.

"No," she thought, "that isn't fair. I broke Vi's, so I s'pose . . ." Hurriedly she tucked the broken clothespin in the go-cart seat. Then she bent down and gently propped her own groom next to Viola's bride. She blinked fast to keep the tears from falling and turned away.

"At least if I can't have a groom, I'll have a maid

of honor," she thought, as she wheeled the go-cart away from the burdock leaf and back to the hollyhocks. "Her dress should be that deep deep pink back there." She hitched herself forward in the go-cart and stretched out, but she couldn't reach far enough. She was about to call for help when a tiny blossom near the top of the stem caught her eye.

"Perfect for a flower girl!" she decided. "Must have opened this morning, it's so small." The tiny blossom was almost white with the faintest touch of pink on the fluted edge of the petals. She stretched as high as she could, pulled it loose and made it a tiny headdress. When the flower girl was finished, Alice turned.

"I can't reach . . ." she called to Vi. But Vi wasn't there. She was over in the sun on the other side of the yard, picking clover blossoms.

"Bet I can do it myself anyhow," Alice thought. She swung her feet off the go-cart footrest and stood by pushing on the arms of the go-cart. She hopped forward one hop, supporting all her weight on her good leg. Then she lowered her other foot to the ground and reached forward to pick the deep ruby red flower. But it hung there—tantalizingly still out of reach. Without thinking at all Alice stepped forward

201

onto the right leg—the leg that ached so much and was so useless. She curved her hand gently around the jewel-like blossom and pinched it free.

Not until she turned with the blossom in her hand did she understand—she had stood on her bad leg . . . and it had held her up! She swayed dizzily and turning plunked heavily in the go-cart once more.

"Ma!" she cried. "Pa!" Her heart pounded and her stomach churned. The rippled edges of the ruby flower in her hand trembled.

Pa hurried around the corner of the house, and Ma pushed up the window. "What is it? What's the matter?" Pa cried.

Alice gulped. "I stood on my leg . . . and it held me up! Oh Pa, I can walk!"

In an instant he was at her side, kneeling by the go-cart and hugging her fiercely. "Are you sure?" he asked. "Can you do it? Ma, did you hear?"

"I heard," Ma answered, running across the grass with Larry in her arms. "It's a miracle! It's God's miracle."

That word again. Miracle. Pa had said, "It'll be a miracle if she walks." And in the spring when the hurricane had come through Sandy Hollow Farm, Ma had used that word. The house hadn't blown down, and no one had been hurt. "Luck," Vi had said. "No," Ma had answered, "It's a miracle." And before that, when the strange black horse had reared and the baby hadn't fallen . . .

"Can you do it now?" Vi said. "Really? Can you?" She waved a fistful of clover blossoms in her excitement.

Alice put her hands on the go-cart arms and stood with her weight on her good leg. Then, as she had before, she put the other foot forward. She shifted her weight—holding her breath. The bad leg worked again! It wobbled a little, and it hurt, but she didn't fall.

All at once, standing there on both legs and shaking with excitement, Alice understood. Miracle. Something God gives you that you don't expect— don't even deserve. Something special. She looked around at Ma and Pa and Viola and Larry.

"I can walk. And I'll be able to run again. I can go to school. I can even be your helper in the barn, Pa. I'll be grown up."

Pa cleared his throat. "You already are grown up. You learned about patience—about being able to wait for the Lord. You learned about faith, and you learned to care about others. That's a lot of learnin' for a little *Svenska flicka*." He turned to Ma, and his voice was husky. "Praise the Lord!" Then he took a deep breath.

"By jingo," he cried, "this calls for a celebration! Let's take the afternoon off from workin' . . ."

"And let's make ice cream!" Viola chimed in. "Oh, Pa, let's!"

"We'll do it," he said. "Nothin' tastes better than our own homemade ice cream. And after all," he smiled at Alice and twirled a moustache point, "miracles should be celebrated!"